Hey, Good Morning, How Are You?

MARTINA HEFTER

Translated by Linda L. Gaus

FIG TREE
an imprint of
PENGUIN BOOKS

FIG TREE

UK | USA | Canada | Ireland | Australia
India | New Zealand | South Africa

Fig Tree is part of the Penguin Random House group of companies
whose addresses can be found at global.penguinrandomhouse.com

Penguin Random House UK,
One Embassy Gardens, 8 Viaduct Gardens, London sw11 7bw

penguin.co.uk

First published in German as *Hey guten Morgen, wie geht es dir?* by Klett-Cotta 2024
First published in Great Britain as *Hey, Good Morning, How Are You?* by Fig Tree 2026

001

Copyright © Martina Hefter, 2024
Translation copyright © Linda L. Gaus, 2026

The moral right of the copyright holders has been asserted

The translation of this book was supported by a grant from the Goethe-Institut.

The work on this novel was supported by a scholarship from the
Cultural Foundation of the Free State of Saxony

Set in 12.1/15.2pt Dante MT Pro
Typeset by Six Red Marbles UK, Thetford, Norfolk
Printed and bound in Great Britain by Clays Ltd, Elcograf S.p.A.

The authorized representative in the EEA is Penguin Random House Ireland,
Morrison Chambers, 32 Nassau Street, Dublin D02 YH68

A CIP catalogue record for this book is available from the British Library

ISBN: 978-0-241-77268-3

Penguin Random House is committed to a sustainable future
for our business, our readers and our planet. This book is made from
Forest Stewardship Council® certified paper.

PRAISE FOR HEY, GOOD MORNING, HOW ARE YOU?

'Completely unflinching . . . Hefter entertains and confronts
you with both expert precision and restrained heart'
Roxy Dunn, author of *Wants and Needs*

'It thrums with energy and excitement . . . A brilliant novel'
Grace Murray, author of *Blank Canvas*

'Laconic and truthful, melancholic and witty . . . In
meticulously crafted language, Hefter's novel asks questions
about time, and about living a good life, without pathos,
and with precise sharpness' *der Freitag*

'So quiet and fine and so sculpted; so sure-footed on a sentence
level; as light as a feather: you can tell it was written by a poet, but
also by a dancer and performer' *Das Literarische Quartett*

'Every line is ready to tear down the austere façade of society'
Dinçer Güçyeter, winner of the 2023 Leipzig Book Fair Prize

'A humorous yet profound prism of privileges, caring for
seriously ill dependents, and the precariousness facing freelance
artists . . . But this isn't the novel's only strength; the way
Hefter tells this story is incredibly humorous without
ever being cynical' *Spiegel Kultur*

'A book that weaves atmospheric nuances into haunting images of
tragedy and bliss, never slipping into sentimentality' *NZZ*

'Primal experiences like loneliness, longing and love
characterize this novel [. . .] The ending leaves readers astonished,
like a great magic trick. How did the author manage to
write a book that is so moving and existential but also
incredibly entertaining?' *Bayerischer Buchpreis*

'The novel's great strength is its lightness. Hefter evokes the
disparate everyday interplay of physical decline and romantic
longing so entertainingly and elegantly that every detail
begins to sparkle through her narrative art' *mdr*

Trailer

Zoom in on a person's back, a big backpiece: 'Exploitation', a looping, somewhat baroque font; there are a few crows flying around the outside.

Cut.

Zoom to another backpiece with the same word, a different font, more angular, the lines not filled out, behind it a sunrise over a river.

Next zoom: 'Exploitation holds the world together', lengthwise along a leg, from top to bottom, a muscular leg, but slim; it's more than one metre long.

A few bees buzz around the text. Bees, who give people honey and work hard for it. The queen in their midst.

It's one of Juno's legs, but the tattoo is a fake; a hand with a facecloth enters the picture, wipes the slogan away.

Zoom to Juno's real tattoos. There are nine. A butterfly; more precisely, a peacock butterfly. Three different deer. The word 'euphoria' with four small butterflies fluttering around it. A dancer in a flowing dress. An open Gothic umbrella made of black lace. A pattern of roses against a grid of thorns, up top, on her right shoulder.

Furthermore, 'dolce vita' on her right upper thigh. A fine, looping font over a star made of dots.

Nice. Why 'dolce vita'?

> 'Dolce vita' is what everyone wants,
> and at the same time, something people
> despise. You can only get it from the
> death and suffering of others.

Ha ha, true!

Zero

She hadn't slept in a while.

And when she slept, she dreamed of stupid things, like hundreds of little dogs that invaded her apartment, yapping angrily. Soon, she herself became an animal; she stopped cleaning the apartment. The animal was wide awake at night, but not especially active.

She lay on a yoga mat on the floor, a few random abdominal exercises, that was all. Actually, she spent most of the time staring at the ceiling. It was decorated with a stucco relief, several concentric circles with blossoms floating on them. They had been painted over so often that they looked like planets. They circled in their orbits, day and night. It was very nice to look at the planets and not much else.

Sometimes, Juno heard the motor of the hospital bed in Jupiter's room humming, then she knew he was still awake, he was adjusting the head of the bed. He had to know if she went to the bathroom or into the kitchen to get a glass of water. But Jupiter never asked questions, and how could she have answered him anyway?

I can't sleep because everything's too much for me. Something like that. First of all, that was wrong, and second, it wouldn't have explained anything.

★

Sometimes she picked up her phone and opened Instagram. She never looked at the feed first; it was usually boring. Instead, she went right into the direct messages. A glittering, bouncing curiosity. Was there another message from Unknown? In that case, the word *Requests* was boldfaced and blue. It was boldfaced and blue almost every night.

Hi beautiful / Hello cutie / Hi sunshine, how are you?

The ones who wrote to her were called Jimmy Taylor_354 or Marcus DeBuonaventura. Their names were PhilGibson1973. William_____Smith and Dr Antonio Alessandro. Suntanned men standing in front of yachts; white, grey-haired men with baseball caps and three-day-old beards.

A cowboy in boots, posing in front of a ranch. A US Army general in his dress uniform. A widower with two children, making pancakes in a luxurious kitchen.

In reality, young men sitting in an internet café somewhere far away, typing kitschy lies into a computer or a phone. Juno had seen a YouTube documentary about this; it was called 'love scamming'. It seemed to be a good business. You wrote to older, apparently single women using a fake profile.

I saw your profile picture and was spellbound right away.
Then the love scammers initiated a relationship.
Good morning, my dear.
What have you eaten today? Take care of yourself.
I love you.
Stickers with red roses, stickers with coffee cups that said 'love'.

A young man was filmed reading a book about psychological manipulation.

I miss you so. I dream of spending my life with you.

At some point, the love scammers asked the women for money.

I'm on a business trip and I had an accident; now I'm sitting here in jail, and I can't access my bank account. Can you help me out?

Juno was simultaneously shocked and fascinated by how many women there were who believed talk like this. The people in the documentary candidly told of the sums these women had transferred to faraway countries via Western Union.

And now she too was on their radar, she of all people, Juno Isabella Flock. Juno, the wife of Jupiter, but the love scammers didn't know anything about that. Undeterred, they showered her with messages. And Juno liked to answer.

In the dark, glittering euphoria of wakefulness, long past midnight, from her room with the planets on the ceiling.

> Hi beautiful lady.
>
>> Hi.
>
> How are you, how's the weather where you are?
>
>> I'm doing very well, thank you.
>> It's 112 degrees here, your brain just
>> melts. What are you up to?
>
> I work for a construction company, ARCO,
> but I'm also a financial adviser. What do you do?
>
>> I'm feeding my falcons, I have three,
>> each one is worth $20,000. Their names
>> are Leo, Bubbo and Lucas.
>
> Wow, that sounds interesting!

Middle-aged white man, grey hair, wearing shorts, standing
under a palm tree.
White man, grey hair, leaning on a convertible.
Sun-kissed white man cuddling a fluffy white dog.
California sailor man, greying Marine with stolen identity.
Come to Juno. She wants to play with you.

> Hi, thank you, I'm doing well.
> I live in Germany, a country with giant
> seal pools in its zoos.
>
> What do I do? I lie in the bath, drink
> liquor, like everyone in Germany.
> I smoke euro notes, have you ever
> tried that?
>
> Are you married? Nope, I live with three
> servants, two men and a woman, we
> berate each other while drinking a case
> of beer.
>
> And you?

For a long while, the love scammers simply believed every-
thing she said. First, it was fun: lying to a guy after midnight.
She reached out her hand: come to me.
It was funny in a mean kind of way.
Sometimes they hesitated.

> Are you serious?
> *Smiley*

How they stumbled, became insecure.

How something crashed into their world, debris from Juno Isabella Flock, who didn't smoke euro notes but instead lived in a room next to Jupiter, who lay in a hospital bed at night. This hospital bed looked like a bed in an actual hospital, except it was covered with contact paper that's supposed to look like wood veneer. During the day, Jupiter sat in a wheelchair. The wheelchair was painted a shiny red; Jupiter picked it out himself way back when. Now there were a few scratches in the paint.

Every morning, he got out of bed and into the wheelchair; this took five minutes. First, Jupiter pushed himself to the edge of the bed, with his legs out front, then lowered first one then the other side of his body down onto the seat, supporting himself with his hands on the armrests.

Jupiter once said, Someone should just lift up the Earth for a moment, that's not so hard.

Perhaps the men who wrote to her deserved to be taken in so easily by Juno. Just as the women that they were deceiving fell for their bullshit.

Was she trying to avenge these women? Probably not.

She couldn't sleep at night any more, that was all.

The love scammers in their third-world countries didn't know anything at all about her, otherwise they probably wouldn't have written to her. She, who lay awake so long at night staring at the ceiling.

Hey, beautiful lady, what are you doing?

Juno answered quickly and effectively. How she was doing and what she was up to. That she'd been married twice and was now whiling away her time with a boring internist.

That she raised attack dogs.

That she loved dogs – wait, that was not a lie.

At some point she noticed that little truths were slipping into her lies. Something that was true. This made Juno uncomfortable rather than amazed. Sometimes it felt good to tell the truth.

Hi beautiful!

How's the weather where you are?

The weather is grey and cold,
November, not a good month. Yesterday
I watched a film, *Melancholia*, have you
seen it? A planet crashes into the Earth,
it doesn't end well. There are two sisters,
Claire and Justine. Once, Justine says
it's good if the world is destroyed, and
Claire can't believe her ears. How can
you be so cold, Justine, hey, we're dying
here and you think that's okay? Or
when Claire realizes that she can't trust
John. John is Claire's husband, a hobby
astronomer. John says Melancholia will
pass by the Earth, don't worry. John is
wrong, the planet comes back, turns
around. Claire's panic, Justine's calm
shortly before the planet hits. Claire
hugs her boys protectively in the garden.

Melancholia, isn't that a nice name for
a stray planet? I like to listen to the film
score when I'm out walking. Sometimes
I think like Justine; a collision like that

with a planet or comet, and that would
be the end.

The love scammer didn't answer.

John gives Claire a wire loop, she can
hold it up against Melancholia in the
garden. Melancholia is hanging in the
daytime sky, a big moon. Claire sees how
it's getting smaller and smaller in the
loop; she thinks it will pull back away
into outer space, she's happy. But just
a day later, Melancholia is much larger
than the loop. Melancholia came back.

How the birds plummet, hail thunders
through the air, the grass trembles.
Threats from outer space always make
me especially sad because they're so
much bigger.

The love scammer didn't read the message.

Hey, write me back, okay?
It's nice to tell you all of this.

The love scammer didn't read the message.

Hey, good morning, how are you?

The love scammer stopped answering.

★

Next guy, the fun continued.

> I like romantic films that don't have a
> happy ending, for example, *Open Water*,
> have you seen it?
> A couple float in the water, they had
> booked a diving trip on the open
> sea, there were several people on the
> boat, the crew miscounts and the
> boat returns to the harbour, forgets to
> collect them.
> They're floating in the Pacific, he is
> attacked by a shark. She has to be
> strong, to comfort him, but he dies in
> her arms. She takes another breath, dives
> down, and never surfaces again.
> I always regarded it as a brutally forceful
> love story. How they have each other,
> hold onto each other, carry each other.
> He holds her so that she can sleep, that's
> when the shark comes.
> I like the implications and the fact that
> the film doesn't sanitize reality.
> Only this way can it actually be a
> romantic film.

The scammer had become unimportant while she was typing
this, although at that point he tried to step in.

> Yes, my dear, true love is something wonderful!
> *Red heart*

> I always think it's great when the truth
> of true love is only revealed in death.

Please don't say such things, dear!

> But it's exactly this kind of thing that
> I want to say.
> In the end, it's death that unites us.
> I'm happy to share that with you,
> by the way.

Bitch.

That's how the chats ended every time.

At some point, the scammers stopped answering and this one got aggressive. Juno wasn't even angry with him. She spoke exactly the same way when she was feeling slightly aggressive as she did when she was being honest.

Sometimes it seemed to her that this was her most sincere self.

It was possible that she was the real Juno in the chats.

ONE

Juno. Names that end in an *o* sound like thunder when it rolls down the slopes of high mountains. Or like deep sleep might sound. Like a sad sigh that someone in this deep sleep emits. Juno, that also sounds like something that repeats itself over and over. Two syllables, spoken endlessly one after the other, an audible GIF.

She had travelled to the mountains for a few days, to the place where she grew up. She was staying with her mother, in the same small apartment right underneath the roof, and sleeping in her childhood bedroom, which was now a room for everything and nothing. Under the diagonal wood walls, it felt like you were in a tent.

On the very first evening, the usual: Juno lay on her back on the floor, as she did at home, looked out of the window at the dark peaks of the Alps outside. Eleven o'clock, twelve o'clock, she saw the lights of the hut at the top of Mount Neuner go out, one of the few huts that were open at this time of year. The lights were like the beacon of a lighthouse. Something that had been there for ever and indicated a direction. She heard the TV in the next room; her mother had turned it up loud, she had become a bit hard of hearing. Otherwise, not much was happening.

★

She talked to Jupiter on the phone every day across the mountains.

Are you doing okay, are you coping?

I'm doing fine, said Jupiter through the ether, everything's great.

Jupiter was doing everything at home without her, opening the refrigerator, taking out the butter, the cheese, putting them on a piece of bread, adding some tomatoes, the mini cherry tomatoes that you didn't have to cut, for Jupiter could no longer hold the knife very well.

But when Juno was with him, all of this had a different quality. Jupiter reached for something – knife, coffee pot, plates – which she could reach for him in case of emergency. Juno was Jupiter's safety net, but now they were each alone for five days without one. Juno could fall on a hike, plummet on a descent, and not come back. And Jupiter could also fall. For example, on the slippery tiled floor in the kitchen, he might not be able to get up again, perhaps his phone wouldn't be nearby.

Juno stayed awake as long as she could. She thought she would sense it if something happened. Although she had come here to learn how to sleep again, it's possible that she didn't want that wholeheartedly.

★ ★ ★

On the very first evening, she got another request on Instagram. It was from Owen_Wilson223.

Juno thought for a moment about whether she should block the profile right away; she wanted to sleep. Or look out of the window a little bit. Her mother had long since gone to bed; she could also go into the living room and watch a movie on TV, open a bag of crisps. On the other hand, a love scammer, Fake Owen Wilson, was sitting somewhere out there under the same night sky that lay over the mountaintops here, waiting for her to respond. It was too tempting. Juno opened the profile. As usual, there were only a couple of photos, posted just a few days ago.

A man with five o'clock shadow, around fifty years old; in the first photo, he was wearing a dinner jacket at a reception. You could see a company's logo on the wall behind him. Owen_Wilson223 had an hors d'oeuvre in his hand, he was smiling at the camera.

In the chat window, it said:

> Hi.
> *Smiley*

Juno clicked *Accept request.*

> Hi!
> *Smiley*

Not even two minutes later, Owen Wilson was online.

> How are you?
>
> > I'm doing fine, and you?
>
> I'm doing splendidly!
> *Smiley with heart-eyes*
> Where do you live?
>
> > I live in Romania, the land of Dracula.
> > Are you familiar with it?
> > And you?

My name is Owen, I'm from Ukraine,
but I live in Austin, Texas!

> Wow, great!
> Are you a cowboy now?
> Did you have to flee because of the war?

Do you have children?

> No, no children, but three dogs.

Wow!
Wow smiley

> Actually, I'm not doing well at all.
> I'm in the mountains now. Each
> morning the sun tumbles out from
> behind the fog and lights up the
> mountains, but it's a little too much of a
> good thing.

> Somehow you see the vulnerability of
> the Earth.

Okay, Lol!
Laughing smiley
Are you married?

> It doesn't matter whether I'm married.
> And just so it's clear: I only want to
> write my thoughts here. Something
> about vulnerability.
> Astronauts always say in interviews
> that the vulnerability of the Earth is

astonishingly visible from space. That
Earth is so small and tender. They were
all shocked what kinds of bad things are
happening on this tender planet.

You're funny, Lol!
Two laughing-crying smileys

Waving grass flies through the wind, the
horses in the barn roll their eyes but they
are quiet.
I've tried to write a poem.
About the film *Melancholia*, a planet is
called that in the film. It comes from the
depths of space, flies out of its orbit and
trundles around, it will hit the Earth.
Have you seen the film?

Longer pause, no response.

And you're not Owen Wilson from
Texas anyhow. You're a love scammer in
an internet café.
And I'm not from Romania.
How I'm doing? If you'd really like
to know:
I'm doing badly because I can't fall asleep.

No response for five minutes.
Juno expected him to block her right away.

You probably think that's a first-world
problem, don't you?

After another five minutes, the speech bubble popped back up.

I like your poem about the horse.

Brief pause.

How do you know about the scammers?

Who can take something like that
seriously?
Owen Wilson from Ukraine, and
your stupid profile photo. All the
schmaltz too.

Are you angry with me?

No, I didn't fall for your act.

Okay.

Are you angry with me?

No. Do you do drugs?

No, why, should I?

I smoke grass.

Grass gives me the giggles.

That's good!
Laughing-crying smiley

I don't think it's good.

Laughter is good.

Sometimes it is, sometimes it's not.

You shouldn't think so much.

I can't stop.

Perhaps you'd rather sleep now?

No one, except perhaps Jupiter, would ever find out that she couldn't sleep any more.

Five more days until her return to Leipzig.

In the small places in the big city, in her little room with the planets and in the room next door, where the hospital bed and wheelchair stood.

The room with a beating heart; Jupiter's heart, which abided there.

Juno set her phone aside and climbed onto the fold-out sofa that had once been in the living room. She was actually a little tired, and the slightly euphoric restlessness, the many ideas and thoughts circling in her head at this hour, which were like foreign starships or birds, weren't there today. Perhaps sleep would come. Owen_Wilson223 supposedly promised to watch over this sleep in the mountains, which was yet to come. While she, Juno Isabella Flock, would watch over Jupiter's sleep from far away, under the stars.

Good morning, were you able to fall asleep yesterday?

Yes, thank you, I managed.

She didn't write anything else just yet.

Her intention was to hike a lot; perhaps that would help with her sleep. The first few days it was foggy, not hiking weather.

You couldn't see the peaks, just the black pine forests below the cliffs. Go to the indoor swimming pool instead, said her mother, but Juno didn't want to swim. Once, she walked through the Vils River valley. A narrow, bumpy path, the first mountain peaks rose up gently to the left and right. She came here often on her own as a child, to play, secretly, for it was too far away from home and also dangerous. Her parents would never have allowed it.

The Vils River flowed parallel to the path, a mountain river that had been straightened and put into a stone straitjacket further downstream, in the town. Here, it raced boisterously and threw itself into bubbling rapids. In the quiet spots, it was deep turquoise and had broad gravel banks. Juno had often ventured secretly into the water there in the summers and swum a few strokes, alone and unobserved, despite all the prohibitions.

Even later on, she had never told anyone about this, neither her parents nor Jupiter. They were here together, right at the start, when they hadn't been together long and were spending a weekend with Juno's parents. Even then, Jupiter couldn't walk very well; he had to take breaks often, the hike took a long time. Juno just thought that he wasn't especially athletic. There wasn't anything disturbing about it. The river was quiet now, normal for this time of year.

The fact that she had swum here alone as a child was like a special secret. Having a secret was like hoarding a little treasure somewhere, buried deep in the earth under a tree; and only Juno knew the spot.

She didn't see her mother that much since her mother was often on the go. In the afternoons, they drank tea together sometimes, herbal mixtures that tasted like wood, pepper or pine needles. You should take this tea along for Jupiter, said her mother; it won't cure him, but it will make him happier, and she promised to pack up some for Juno. As long as she could remember, her mother had gathered all the herbs in the mountains and dried them on the balcony. Whenever Juno fell down as a child and scraped her knee or hurt her hand, her mother rubbed the spots with home-made arnica tincture. It always helped.

Will the tea also make me happier? asked Juno, and her mother said that no tea in the world could help her. She was trying to make a small, tender joke; you could hear that from her tone of voice. But then they were both silent for a moment.

That's probably right, said Juno.

★ ★ ★

The sky cleared on the third day. Juno photographed the snowy mountain peaks from the balcony; they were snow white in front of a baby-blue sky. Now the town looked much bigger. And suddenly the nights were giant and high; the Milky Way spread its stars all across the mountains.

She had a message every evening.

> What's it like in the mountains?
> How high are the mountains?
> Hi, what are you doing right now?

> > It's beautiful, lonely, windy; at the
> > moment, everything's a bit precipitous.
> > Sometimes I think it's like being on
> > Mars. I go hiking in the morning; there's
> > a moor with a beaver.

> I like beavers, the way they pursue their
> goals so busily, without asking why.

Lol. I like the way you write.
You're funny.
Laughing-crying smiley

Smiley

She didn't believe that Owen Wilson was writing to her as himself now, without a purpose, without an ulterior motive.

Wherever she looked, the devils were there first.

In the documentary about love scamming, she had seen that exposed scammers still tried to approach their victims, in other ways, with other lies. She considered blocking the profile now after all. Just a click and goodbye. But she had already sent too many responses, too many of her words were in the atmosphere. Was it possible to pull them back?

Of course she was still lying a bit.

This time intentionally, for who knows with whom she was actually interacting.

> Actually, I live in Chemnitz.
> I'm on holiday right now.
> A cute little city with a lot of fountains
> and a castle.
> No, I don't have any children, I can't
> even cook.

(which was true)

★

She didn't say anything about Jupiter; she wrote that she lived alone.

That she lived from affair to affair, always taking new lovers. She made herself three years younger and wrote that she was an actress. Which was approximately what she would have liked to have been.

> I'm only really there when I'm on stage.
> Then I exist.

(and that was also true)

> I still go to a lot of parties because what else should you do? I like my life.

(debatable)

He was familiar with her Instagram profile. Perhaps also her real name. He could google. She didn't live in Chemnitz. He could probably find out some things about her. Photos of past performances in Leipzig theatres, programme announcements. And even three interviews, two on national radio and one on local cultural radio.

Juno Isabella Flock. Her traces were all over.

* * *

In the nights that followed, they spent a lot of time on their phones, typing into the speech bubbles, even though Juno didn't want to at first. Chatting so much was something she'd never liked to do; it always gave her a stiff neck.

The dark wood of the balcony threw additional darkness

through the window; she turned on a small orange lamp, held her phone right next to her face.

He told her that he lived in Nigeria. In a medium-sized city in the south-west.

Juno didn't look at Google Maps, because she knew: he was pretty far away.

She also learned his real name: Benu.

Juno looked the name up later on. Benu was a figure in ancient Egyptian mythology, a type of precursor to the phoenix, a god of the dead. Benu spent the night in the Duat, the realm of the dead, and in the morning light he was reborn as a heron.

Juno liked the name. It, like *Juno*, ended in something dark; like *Juno*, it had just two syllables.

If you repeated the syllables without a pause, at some point they sounded like one continuous sound.

Once, far enough away, high enough up to be so direct, she asked Benu about scamming. Why he did it. She thought her question seemed factual and genuinely interested.

No police, please.

That, by contrast, seemed very urgent.

He would like to stop, but he had no choice.

The police are brutal here,
jail is hardcore.

You know best what you're doing.
But don't worry, I won't turn you in.
I wouldn't even know where.
Smiley

'Hello, good day, police district in (Nigerian city south-east of Lagos). This is Juno Isabella Flock. There's a love scammer in your city, his name is Benu, could you please put him in jail? Thank you.'

Go ahead and write to women who are dumb enough to fall for that. The main thing is that I have a counterpart.

She didn't write that, didn't even want to think that, but she thought it anyway. For outer space was on fire, and the little dogs that sometimes still populated her dreams were dancing around like crazy.

You could only share something like that with someone who was far enough away.

Are you listening? Scammer Benu?

★ ★ ★

Nigeria. Juno had to think where exactly in Africa the country was, and she was ashamed that she didn't know for sure. Somewhere more to the left, not all the way down. She booted up her computer, looked at Google Maps; that was about right. Still.

Then she looked for the city where Benu lived. She had never heard the name. It was a little way inland from the coast; the Niger River flowed just over one hundred miles further west.

She knew almost nothing about Nigeria. Once she had read a report about street artists in Lagos in the *Frankfurter Allgemeine Zeitung*; it had impressed her. She remembered a photo, a few young men standing around in a mixture of native dress, rags and punk costumes; in front of them were two hyenas bound by giant iron chains. The hyenas were kept

25

like circus animals; it was said that the men strolled through the quarter with them, making the hyenas do tricks. The hyenas wore muzzles of knotted rope, Juno remembered that, and that she had thought how afraid she would be of these animals. And then she remembered 'Boko Haram'; for a while the news was full of horror stories about them.

When was that again? She remembered those girls. Kidnapped from a school because they were girls who went to school.

Juno checked on her computer; it was 2014.

Two hundred and seventy-six schoolgirls from the Chibok Girls State Secondary School were taken away in trucks by alleged security forces in the middle of the night and dragged into the forest along the border with Cameroon. Ninety-six girls, now women, were still missing. Eleven women escaped in June 2022; they had all borne several children and found in some cases that their parents had died. It's been a while since we heard anything about that in Europe, thought Juno.

And the story wasn't over yet.

One evening, she was chatting with Benu about Nigeria.

> Tell me something about your country.

That was what the other love scammers had always asked her, and she answered that people ate rose petals for breakfast.

> It's a bit bleak here.
> The north is dangerous, nobody wants to go there.
> Most people move to Lagos at some point.

I have no work, I sit around all day, at most I do my laundry.

(By hand, Juno asked.)

I live with my mother.

(He said he was thirty-two.)

I help her with the housework,
sometimes anyway.
Winking smiley
Most of the time I'm bored.
I play some video games, smoke grass.

Meanwhile, they were messaging on WhatsApp and not via Benu's scammer profile. Bye-bye, Owen Wilson. Juno saw his profile picture. His real picture, not the greying Mr Wilson.

He looked friendly, a little older than thirty-two. Sometimes panic flared within her. Who knew who was really behind this phone sending his waves across to her little town in the Alps. If the waves could come this far, perhaps Benu could as well.

What else did he write?

That he liked listening to her. That he had to laugh at her sentences, they were special. That he found her funny.

Oh. Her heart leapt for a moment. She felt flattered. But surely this was just one of the usual love scammer tricks. He only said it to get something.

He wanted to get close enough to her that she would think it was real. Just as Melancholia came close to Earth and you could see the craters, like on the moon. She wrote back that this pleased her. Then she wrote that she would be out of touch for the next few days; she wanted to take a longer excursion to a mountain hut. No internet, she needed peace and quiet for a change.

The truth was that nobody would spend a few days in a mountain hut in November. Most mountain huts were closed in November. She just needed a break from him.

Everything had moved too fast, and the game had taken a different turn than usual. Juno had guessed that Benu would soon block her or stop writing to her. Like the other scammers, when they recognized that they couldn't get anything from her and that she was only stealing their time.

But now, they were in the middle of the game.

TWO

A foggy winter had Germany in its grasp.

In Leipzig, grey light hung over the streets by day, and in the evening, the streetlights lit the sky up in orange. The stars were hidden; even when the sky was clear, there were hardly any to be seen.

Orion was visible from the northern hemisphere; from Europe, it was upright or slightly tilted. With a little imagination, you could make out a figure in these stars. The figure was drawing a bow and had no head, or only a very small one, consisting of just one star.

In ancient Egypt, people saw Osiris in this constellation. The Sumerians saw a sheep.

How was insomnia any different from looking at the constellations and knowing that you have some kind of roof or shelter over your head? Constellations were an interface between science and mythology. They displayed people's touching fantasy and their enormous knowledge. People used the constellations for navigation and researched their individual stars; some of them were very young, some very old.

How was insomnia different from becoming euphoric about all of this? It was dangerous to devote yourself so fully to it. Not sleeping was unhealthy, it robbed you of your bodily resources. But it was hers alone.

* * *

Sleep had returned for a short while during her stay in the mountains; the euphoria of being awake had given way to lackadaisical slumber, which Juno almost let wash over her against her will. Now, not even two weeks later, everything was as it had been. Sometimes Juno thought that dancing was for her what sleep was for other people.

She knocked quickly on Jupiter's door, entered in a rush without pausing.

Ciao, Jupi, see you later! A quick, waving hand thrown in his direction, then she was out of the room again.

Jupiter sat in his wheelchair, had opened his computer.

Please take the letter with you, he said, and he took an envelope from the bedside table.

Juno was familiar with this routine. The envelope contained Jupiter's health insurance card; she had to send it to Jupiter's neurologist so that he could get the prescription for the next three months' supply of Copaxone by mail. The card came back in an envelope with the prescription.

Initially, Jupiter had made his way to the doctor's office every three months, leaning on his walking aids, travelling two stops by tram, but he hadn't been able to do that for a while now. How long exactly?

Jupiter couldn't travel alone in his wheelchair. It was electric like an e-bike, but also very difficult to manoeuvre. The footpath to the tram was pocked with holes and dents. And to make matters worse, the old pavements had high kerbs and were lowered in only a few places. And, of course, that's precisely where the cars were parked. Without help,

Juno also couldn't carry the wheelchair down the eight steps from the front door of their building to the pavement.

For a while, she went to the doctor's office to pick up the prescription herself, but increasingly she only managed this at the last moment. At some point, Jupiter had called the office and asked whether it would be possible to send the insurance card in the post.

Juno put the envelope in her bag with her leotard and toe shoes; it got a bit wrinkled, but whatever.

Of course, she said.

She blew a kiss in Jupiter's direction, goodbye again, she wouldn't be home before dark. She went out, down the pavement to the main street. There was some dog poo, the sky splintered a bit, but otherwise things were okay.

★ ★ ★

She had started dancing again in September, in her former ballet studio. She needed this first and foremost for her work, to be able to dance ballet. For body tension. For posture. In her body, ballet was like a special costume that fitted everything, regardless of what she did in her performances.

During the pandemic, she trained mostly by herself, outdoors in the alluvial forest or in her room, from which she had removed most of the furniture, shifting it to the small room next door. For a while, it was really nice to dance alone. But when the pandemic was finally over, Juno noticed that she missed the discipline; just like insomnia, it elicited euphoria in her body. The small impulses from the outside, other people's eyes on her body, and also the communal energy that formed like an invisible cloud during a class, wrapping itself around all of them.

Everyone from back then was still there: Naïs, Athena,

Daphne, Ursi. When Juno came back to the studio for the first time, they all said hello. You're still alive, old girl? Wow, you haven't changed a bit!

They hugged each other for a long while, Juno remembered that well. None of them were so young any more; maybe that's why they hugged each other so tightly. They wanted to protect themselves against that final parting.

Naïs, the teacher, had just turned fifty, but you wouldn't know that from looking at her. She had been a soloist in several opera houses, and she still leapt so quickly that you might think she was floating on air. Athena, just two years younger than Juno, was a pianist and had been doing ballet since she was five. As had Daphne and Ursi, plus there were two new faces.

When someone asked Juno how often she danced, she told them the truth. Then most people looked a little shocked.

Six days a week, Monday to Saturday.

In truth, Juno was Nijinsky.

Wings on her feet, a knife in her belt.

* * *

It was already almost nine o'clock when she got home, and she unpacked the sweaty dance clothes from her bag. She put the whole lot in the washing machine, wanted to shower right away. Then she held Jupiter's letter in her hands. The paper had softened on one side, perhaps from her sweaty leotard.

She had forgotten the letter. It wasn't the first time.

Juno went into the kitchen, to the fridge, where the syringes with the Copaxone had to be stored. There were still three syringes there. If she sent the letter tomorrow, the prescription would come in four days at the earliest. Copaxone was essential for Jupiter; he had taken a shot each day since 2008.

A few weeks ago, Juno had calculated how many shots that was so far, and she had tried to imagine how many dustbins full of empty syringes that made. She had taken all of these dustbins out to the larger bins in the courtyard because Jupiter hadn't been able to do that for a long time. She decided that she would go to the doctor's office on the dot of eight o'clock the next morning, give them the letter and pick up the prescription right away; that would be safer.

Hi, Jupi, she said through the glass door. Is everything okay?

Everything's fine, called Jupi.

She heard the keyboard clicking, Jupiter was writing something. She knocked and went in and sat down on the sofa; they began talking about something. How dancing was (good), how the air outside was (cold), what kind of mood the people outside were in (Juno didn't know).

She didn't say anything about the letter. That it was still in her bag, a light weight, perhaps twenty grams. Then they talked a little bit about the new insect hotel.

Jupiter had bought an insect hotel online. It had been on the sill in front of the window for a few days, a little wooden house with tubes of different sizes built into it.

What kind of insects would move in there? asked Juno, and Jupiter said, Perhaps butterflies or wasps.

Hopefully they'll all get along well, said Juno.

Only when she had stood up again and wanted to leave the room did Jupiter ask if she'd sent the letter.

Juno stopped briefly in the doorway, turned back towards

Jupiter. He was concentrating on the screen again; that made it a little easier.

Of course I did, said Juno.

Later on, she did a few more stretches on the woollen blanket. It was still early enough, you could hear people passing in front of the window every now and then. It was the hour before life gets really quiet, between evening and night.

She could go outside like the night owls sweeping by under her window, she could listen to music with her earbuds in and cry. Sometimes she really liked to do that, to cry on the street. Frequently uninhibited, when there was really nobody around, then she just let the tears fall. If people were approaching, it was good sport to stop crying in time. You had to take a deep breath, relax your face and look at something stupid; a dustbin or a parked car on the street, and that was all.

A message from Benu popped up.

Hey, how are you doing, what are you doing?

Hi, I'm doing well, thanks.
I'm lying on the floor
looking at the ceiling.

She sent a photo of the stucco relief.

Once upon a time, the spheres were
flowers. They've been painted over so
often that now they look like planets in a
solar system, don't you think?

That's a nice pattern.

> There's stucco on the ceiling nearly
> everywhere here.

She had to look up the word for 'stucco' in English in Google Translate.

> I live in a country where you can stare
> at your stucco ceiling for weeks and
> nobody will notice.

What exactly do you mean?

> Oh, it doesn't matter.

What have you done today?

> I was dancing and forgot to post a letter.

Something important?

> Yes, but I'll take care of it first thing
> tomorrow.

Sticker: Four dancing letters: GOOD!
The 'g' a face with a laughing mouth.

> When I was a child, I once rode the
> school bus for six months with fake
> monthly tickets.
> My parents had to fill out a form, I
> was supposed to take it to school and I
> forgot. The form stayed in my schoolbag
> for weeks, and I didn't have a ticket,
> somehow no one noticed.

The tickets were made of thin paper,
with a red stamp with the month
and year.
I got expired tickets from a friend and
scraped the stamp off with a razor blade.
Then I wrote the current date on them
with a red felt-tip pen.
I did that for six months without getting
caught. You had to show the tickets to
the bus driver, they never looked too
closely.

And how did you get caught?

At some point, the school called my
parents, asking why they hadn't handed
in the form.

Were they angry?

No, I just kept on lying.
I told them that of course I'd handed
the form in. I didn't dare to say anything
when the tickets didn't come.
Then my parents were mad at the
school, not at me.

Sometimes you have to lie.
That's the only way.
Everyone lies sometimes, even children.

Briefly she thought that it sounded a bit funny when a love
scammer wrote sentences like this. But she also could have
written them.

The question is whether, when you're lying,
you're really lying to yourself.

Once again, there was a short pause, Benu didn't respond.

Like when the planet Melancholia hits
the Earth, and then there's a big fireball,
there's so much beauty in this.
The film is online, you have to watch it.

I've never heard of it.
Maybe I'll do that sometime.
Two smileys

She lived on this planet. Not on the one that was hit, but on
the other one. The planet Melancholia. The one that just
missed Earth the first time but hit it the second.

THREE

Juno Isabella Flock: white woman, lives in Germany.

Privileged.

No children.

Therefore, not quite average in Germany.

Freelance performance artist; sometimes she earns more, sometimes less money.

Hopes that she can work as an artist until the end of her life.

And then falls over dead without much fuss.

Flock is over fifty and thus no longer so privileged.

Before a performance festival in Leipzig, the director of one of the participating theatre groups told her that the festival was really for younger productions.

Flock will survive this.

Flock lives in a beautiful city made of light-coloured stone, with wide streets.

Flock still has about twenty-three years to live if everything goes well.

Flock lives in a tattered nineteenth-century apartment building on a quiet street. The interior doors have glass panels in the middle, they rattle when the wind slams the doors. Earlier inhabitants replaced the original doors with these. The light falls from the outside through the windows, shines right into the rooms.

Jupiter is out there in the hall.

Juno can see him through the glass door of her room.

Jupiter is walking down the hall, leaning on the walker, on his way to the bathroom, to the kitchen. She sees his naked legs through the glass. Jupiter can't put his trousers and socks on so well by himself any more, so sometimes he doesn't wear any. Jupiter doesn't want Juno to help him with his socks.

She and Jupiter can't move into another apartment, one with wooden doors.

Nor into an accessible apartment.

Soon, rents in Leipzig will be as high as they are in Munich.

Their neighbours all have at least one car.

Juno can't sleep any more.

Juno will never again climb mountains or go to the sea with Jupiter.

Juno hates that she is the only one who takes out the rubbish, never Jupiter.

Juno hates herself for hating this.

Juno is confronted with her reality, which she doesn't tell the scammers about, and it's an impenetrable wall.

Be glad, scammers, that Juno lies like this.

Juno is sitting in her light-flooded room looking out, and there's nothing threatening her with imminent death.

The street is a quiet, clean street; there are no dealers, no youth gangs, no drunks hanging around, just people walking their dogs and children making their way to the primary school down the street in the mornings. Then there are only little, happy voices out there.

Parents who accompany their children home in the afternoons, then it's much quieter.

The apartment with its glass doors is secure for the moment.

The glass will not shatter with a clank at night and burst because a bomb falls somewhere nearby.

The water flows smoothly from the taps in the mornings, at midday, at night. Juno is well fed and has heat (even this winter).

And all of this will likely continue for the rest of her life, which from a statistical point of view will probably be about twenty-three years.

This insight doesn't make anything better.

At least not for Juno.

More and more often, she doesn't care if she's crying on the street at night and she sees people coming. Sometimes she wipes tears from her face unapologetically as she's passing through such a happy group.

Should Juno tell the love scammers this? That she's the crying lady of Leipzig-Schleußig?

Then they would just send her their memes, two little dogs hugging each other, or two hands making a heart with their fingers.

Memes that just make you cry more.

Memes with motifs, with which more people than love scammers think that they can make women happy.

She could tell them about Jupiter's hospital bed.

How they worked together to take off the rod with

triangular bar to hold onto at the head of the bed after the men from the medical supply store had set it up. Then, Jupiter was able to stand by himself for a few minutes and hold the bar while Juno took the screws out of the anchor with the electric screwdriver.

He could not sleep under such a bar, said Jupiter. How they just shoved the dismantled rods and the bar under the bed, where the bath seat already lay, a monstrous plastic object that Jupiter was supposed to put on the bathtub and climb into so that he wouldn't slip in the bath when he wanted to shower. But Jupiter couldn't climb into the seat. And the seat was heavy. Juno could not haul it to the bathtub and take it out again.

Somewhere in Plagwitz, one neighbourhood away, someone had sprayed *Truth* on the wall of a building, at least two metres high, lavender and red and blue, in round, dancing letters that seem to light up as you approach them.

The truth is larger than life, like the graffiti, thinks Juno.
Her truth, but also the general, wide-ranging truth.
You can see it from anywhere on Earth.

FOUR

And then it was 2023.

Juno saw the first posters with her image on them in the city: she was standing between Phoebus and Tristan in a decommissioned fountain in the palm garden in Plagwitz, looking into the camera while blinded by the sun, while the men looked up at the sky with nonplussed faces. They took the photo in the spring; the photographer came up with the fountain idea. They looked good, like a band, thought Juno.

Phoebus and Tristan were also a band.

The name of their piece was written in large, neon yellow letters. Below it, somewhat smaller, their names and the name of the theatre, the date, the time.

She showed Jupiter a picture of one of the posters.

Cool, he said.

But strange, said Juno.

What?

That I'm on posters all over the city, and yet I can just barely pay my rent.

But it was actually nice. A small, anticipated rush to see yourself on the posters.

In a few days, it would be time. Three performances in Leipzig, the revival of a performance somewhere between a music show and theatre. In April, there would be three guest performances in Munich. The applications for funding had all been submitted. How crazy, Juno often thought. It was her first own piece, a scenic performance with music, text and costumes, like a musical on steroids. Juno almost didn't care whether it was a good or bad piece. The main thing: she got to be on stage.

Being on stage was like insomnia, you could quickly lose yourself in it. Each theatre was a cabinet of curiosities, in which life didn't take you in one direction, towards death, but rather back and forth and side to side.

Now sometimes she halted briefly in front of the poster: Juno had asked the photographer not to retouch her so that she looked younger, but she didn't see such a great difference between herself and Tristan and Phoebus. And they were in their late thirties at most. That's what was bad about getting older: when you look in the mirror, you look the same, but other people see the difference.

The rehearsals started, the air in the little theatre smelled good, like fleece, chalk and dust. They considered how the lighting design should look; the theatre stage was a black box. More blue, said Tristan; more lavender, said Phoebus; and stage fog, said Tristan; lots of darkness, said Juno; just a few bright spots, and the theatre technician nodded and typed everything they said into his computer and pressed the buttons on his control panel. Sometimes, when they were starting a scene, Juno had the feeling that he was squinting through the light to check something.

Whether she could still do all these things: speak, dance, wear a costume. A hooded jacket with blue spangles, which glimmered in the spotlights.

Whether she was still allowed to do all this at her age,

wear this shimmering jacket. Do a few moves that she had choreographed herself.

Maybe it was ridiculous.

She was a little late getting there. Other freelancers had long since stopped when they were as old as she was. But she had just begun, at least as she saw things.

Phoebus had asked her once what she had done before, and Juno had to think about this. When was before? Ten years ago, when she was in her early forties? Jupiter was already sick then. A few smaller dance jobs here and there, of course also freelance, not in fixed theatres. She lived in part from the disability allowance that Jupiter received. It was also for her, as she was the one who did everything at home: shopping, cleaning, tidying up. And all the other things that you didn't think of at first. The things which apparently could be done quickly and easily, but which added up to more than you might think.

Benu wrote several times each day.

I'm in the theatre, she told him in her first message, saying she couldn't write to him during the day. Juno's phone lay on a chair on the stage; it was set to silent, but with each message there was a short buzz from the seat out into the room, due to the vibration.

There, and there, and there, and again. Signals from far away.

Juno only looked at the messages in the evenings. There were a lot.

What are you doing today?
Are you busy?

I was in the theatre, we're rehearsing for
a show. I'm performing soon, this time
with a band.
Busy, I guess, but that's what I'm doing.

What kind of a band is it?

Two musicians, guitar, synthesizer, bass,
Singing. Everyone in the city knows
them. They play in clubs or on the street.
I just asked them, I absolutely wanted
to create a show where there's a band
playing.

Are they rappers?
I like to listen to hip-hop and blues.

I like those too, but it's more of a kind
of gloomy blues-wave, it's great!

I'd like to make music too.

Why don't you?

I don't know. Too little opportunity. And I can't
play an instrument.

What should she say?
What people in Germany said: go ahead and start?
Get yourself a guitar and go for it?
Or become a rapper.

I'm sorry.
But sometimes it just happens.
You just have to keep your eyes open.

And have courage.

Will you be paid a lot?

Enough.

She had made the usual applications for funding, the Cultural Foundation of the Free State of Saxony, Leipzig cultural office, with extensive designs and costings and a financial plan. The normal self-exploitation in freelance art, if you aren't very famous, and if you want to persist and become an established theatre collective that might receive funding support for design over several years at some point. You had to start early to achieve this. Juno was late on the draw.

Of course she didn't write all of this.

She sent two photos that she had taken one morning during a coffee break. A selfie with the timer; she had leaned her phone on the back of a chair in the auditorium.

Juno in the glittery blue hooded jacket; you saw her only from the back, just an outline in the stage fog that was streaming out of the dry ice machine, wrapping itself around her like a cloud.

Then a photo of the empty stage in the morning, just the instruments standing there, plus her microphone, a little further towards the front of the room. Otherwise, nothing.

Juno thought the photo might give a good impression of what she was doing. The empty stage showed the most precise picture: because nothing had happened yet.

Her very first performance was in a Christmas play when she was in kindergarten. She had the main role; she played a small, crooked pine tree. She was mocked by the tall, straight trees in the forest. St Nicholas came into the forest and was looking for a Christmas tree for heaven, and he chose her, the crooked tree Juno.

Because she had a pure heart, said St Nicholas.

Juno remembered every detail of this performance.

That she liked Jason, who played St Nicholas.

That she had sung a duet with him.

That she had to stand in a crooked position, with her hands high above her head to make the top of the pine tree.

That her mother had cried in her seat.

That when they were leaving the show, other mothers had whispered, 'That's the girl who, whisper, whisper, whisper.'

By then, Juno realized that she hadn't been acting at all.

Instead, things were the other way around. She was only acting when she wasn't standing on a stage. On normal days. Then she was acting at being a normal person.

A normal Juno.

Good night, Benu, she wrote.

She actually liked writing to him.

Later, when she was making herself two scrambled eggs in the kitchen because she was hungry again, a song lyric came to her out of the blue. It was a bad, somewhat cynical line, but it was a kind of unsolicited earworm, and she sang it to herself in her thoughts:

> Germany isn't the land of your dreams
> Guitars here are made of diamonds.
> If I'm really honest, the diamonds
> Mined in Africa aren't what they seem.

Twang, twang, twang.

★ ★ ★

Then came the performances. Three completely sold-out evenings and a lot of applause each time; she had to return to the stage over and over again. It went by much too fast. Then came the bit after the performances.

As usual, the first day was intoxicating, sleeping in and looking at the pictures from the evenings a hundred times and smiling misty-eyed. Then the horrible second day. When you were completely sober again. When the theatre spotlights were finally turned off.

The grandiose normality of the theatre; this real, palpable world gave way to the strange, invented world of everyday life.

At the supermarket, there were strawberries from Chile and other surreal things that just had to be a lie.

Juno wanted to go back.

She saw Benu's messages popping up on the lock screen and glowing unread like small, helpless meteorites diving into Earth's atmosphere.

Benu was just writing to squeeze money out of her in the end; this seemed much too mundane to her.

That was the ugliness of the world. She didn't have a clear head for this.

At some point during a walk, she wrote back that he shouldn't write to her all the time.

He shouldn't think that she was going to send him money one day. And she wrote that.

Why are you always this way?
I'm not messaging you as a scammer.

We'll see.

Was she too mean to him or just realistic?

In the USA, fifty million dollars were sent to African scammers in 2011, said Wikipedia. Meanwhile, the concern was not just money.

Visas were also popular.

You could invite a scammer.

You could marry him.

You could fly a scammer in.

Unfortunately, you can forget it if you're thinking about anything like that.
I don't have the time, money or energy to bring you to Germany. And it's not that easy either. And I have no reason to do that.

It would be nice if you could finally be a bit more trusting.
I don't give a shit about Germany.

It's also not that great here.
It's best to hold onto the stars.
I can see Orion above me, the constellation. You have to see it.
Here down below, on Earth, it looks as if all the stars of a constellation are scattered on the same level. But they are scattered at different depths, some of them probably don't even exist any more. You just see the light; it's like a type of illustration, I think sometimes. You remember someone and just see their light. A little sad, but also beautiful.

It rained here. Did you smoke grass?

In any case, he was honest in what he wrote.

She put in her earbuds and played the *Melancholia* sound-track on Spotify.

There was a glowing sphere in the sky.

But it was just the moon.

A few days later, she sat in front of her laptop, surfing around in the city where Benu lived.

Where did he live, the guy she was chatting with? What did the neighbourhood look like? According to Wikipedia, the city was not all that large; about half a million inhabitants, two universities. It had been a Catholic archdiocese since 1997. The city's football club played in the first Nigerian league; the stadium held ten thousand people.

The weather forecast for twelve o'clock: 100 degrees Fahr-enheit, overcast, likelihood of snow: 0 per cent.

> What I'm doing? I'm sitting at my
> computer, reading something about
> your city.

Really? Lol!

> Why Lol?

I just think it's funny.
Why are you interested in my city?
It's not so spectacular.

> Because I know you.
> But don't think that I'm making any
> travel plans.

Benu asked her for a photo. A current one, right away, a selfie. It was still January.

Milky white or dirty grey sky that just wouldn't clear up. Everything took too long in January.

Jupiter was sleeping a lot. Sometimes Juno noticed that his face was thinner, and the wheelchair looked larger when Jupiter was sitting in it than it had two months ago.

She bought him trail mix because she thought the nuts would do him good, due to the fatty acids. People said they were good for the nerves.

A photo, why? she asked Benu.

Benu had seen at least a few photos from her Instagram profile, when he had written to her as Owen Wilson; those should suffice.

Juno thought she looked ugly in photos, and she always wanted to correct these photos with reality right away, for in reality she still thought she looked ugly, but she could make a gesture that somehow softened her face; where she had a voice, a few sentences and words.

Benu wrote that in the long run, you had to see someone's face frequently to talk to them.

And that was also right. Okay, okay.

She stood next to the floor lamp, checked her hair and what she was wearing: T-shirt, leggings, nothing that could be misconstrued. Then she set her phone on the windowsill and pressed the self-timer button. Of course she didn't smile.

You see, I'm not a bot.

You look funny!
Very special, like a sprite!
Laughing emoji

Juno felt better that Benu wrote this, with the laughing smiley with tears. It would have unsettled her if he had written, You're really beautiful.

Benu sent a photo of himself. He sat in the corner of a room, with a wall painted yellow behind him; you couldn't see anything else.

Also a selfie, you can see the position, the hand with the smartphone out in front, the face slightly from the side.

Benu looked like he did in his profile picture. He was wearing a bright blue T-shirt and smiling.

She had sometimes thought that she looked like a sprite. That was probably because of her eyes, they were very crooked. Her mother said once that her great-great-grandmother came from Siberia and that's why they had those eyes and high cheekbones in this family.

As a child, her hair was platinum blonde, then it passed through medium and dark blonde, now it was nearly brown. But it wouldn't go grey. Her mother didn't have any grey hair either and her father had remained blond until the end of his life; blond, short hair. In the end, when he got sick and had to have chemotherapy, his hair only fell out on top. The hair on the sides remained, became a bright wreath, a decent halo.

She ran her index finger along the contour of her lower jaw. On Instagram, there were reels; they called this contour the jawline and showed you how you could make this jawline look sharper with dark make-up.

Or you could have hyaluronic acid injected there. In another reel, Juno had watched a woman in a lab coat sticking a long tube into the jawline of a woman lying on a table in a doctor's surgery.

She didn't know the word 'jawline' until just a few weeks ago.

Back in her room, she found a message from Benu.

How old are you again?

> I already told you that.
> *Smiley*

She told him her fake age again, the one that she had told him in their first chats.

Three years younger. Those three years didn't make any difference, but the number didn't look as bad.

Really?

> No fake flattery, okay?
> *Smiley with the crooked-line mouth*

No, no flattery.
I just think it's crazy,
you don't look your age.

> I look like most women my age.

First, she wanted to send an emoji.

The rolling-on-the-floor-laughing emoji.

The blue freezing-into-ice emoji.

The red monster emoji.

The skull emoji.

The alien emoji.

The green vampire with medium-long hair.

While she was thinking, her phone's display screen locked. Juno saw her face reflected in the phone's black glass surface. None of the emojis described what she was. She sent the message off without an emoji.

Without feeling, she thought, and she had to smile.

* * *

Shy sun for two or three days, then snow again.
Juno filmed the flakes with her phone.
They blossomed from within themselves.
Up there, that was the sky.
Germany lay in a bad-weather zone.

Most recently, Instagram was showing posts from Nigeria in her feed, probably because of her Google searches. Now she was following an influencer from New York. She did something with fashion; in her photos, she showed clothing or advertised make-up, applied colourful eyeshadow, glued on fake eyelashes.

There was a post with pictures of the airport in New York; the influencer was standing at the gate with two large aluminium suitcases, wearing high platform shoes and a neon pink suit. In the caption, it said that she was travelling to Lagos. First, it wasn't clear what her relationship to Nigeria was, but in another post she said she was flying home.

Later, the woman was standing between two soldiers on a street; behind them were high walls, palms and a lot of green.

Juno read that this was a gated community.

Several slides, the woman posed, the soldiers unmoving, they only changed the position of their guns once.

Then a reel: the woman sat in a restaurant, filming her meal: a plate with pasta and squid and other squiggly-looking appetizers. In the background, you could see the plumes of an indoor fountain. Juno was hungry.

Then the woman was walking through a shopping centre. She filmed clothing in a boutique; you could see high heels on the shelves, cocktail dresses, embroidered all over with sequins. Somehow, it was a familiar picture of a mall, only the people in the aisles and stores weren't white, and there was no Rossmann in sight.

In the comments, someone wrote: Watch out that you don't get kidnapped, with a laughing smiley. Juno had read previously that in Nigeria, especially in rural areas, you could be kidnapped by gangs. Apparently, this happened frequently, not just to rich people. You got kidnapped, the families had to pay, sometimes over the course of weeks. If they didn't have a lot of money, the amounts were small.

And another reel: a drive through Lagos. Sometimes the streets and houses were a little rundown, sometimes very chic, like the new, quickly built luxury area in Leipzig on the White Elster River, 1,150 euros for 50 square metres. The influencer filmed people on the streets from the car window. People partying in an outdoor club, the people waved at the camera and raised their beer bottles. At an intersection, a man in a royal blue suit with coloured stripes danced. Sometimes a military car was visible in the picture; a pick-up truck with soldiers in it. They wore sunglasses and had machine guns on their shoulders.

At some point, Juno landed on the page of the Federal Foreign Office, on the travel warnings. There was a partial travel warning for Nigeria:

In Nigeria, you should never travel overland at night. If you have to travel by land, check the security situation along the route, before and during the trip, and make the trip with an armed escort (mobile police, MoPol). Avoid the Abuja–Kaduna train line; it had been the target of several terrorist attacks.

Avoid crowds of people in cities.

In case of armed attacks, do not resist; hand over all the valuables you have.

Heed curfews.

Follow the instructions of local security forces.

Benu had written that his aunts lived in a village, and he had to go there often. He went by train, the rest by bus, the trip took more than four hours. It was pretty stressful, he wrote, the roads were bad and bumpy.

> I smoke grass, it relaxes me.
> You should smoke grass too.

Yes, maybe she should do that. It would make her hopelessly frazzled. She wouldn't get anything done, perhaps she would only sleep. Did she want that?

Who would take Jupi's letters to the postbox?

In every other chat, Benu wrote that Juno should also smoke grass, it would make everything easier. Sometimes, it seemed like a small accusation and other times like the advice of a good friend.

Had she been to Africa? asked Benu.

No, not yet.

Where have you been?

Austria, Switzerland, Italy, England,
Denmark, Belgium, Poland, Czechia,
Serbia, Hungary, Slovenia and Israel.

Wow-smiley
You really get around!

> That's nothing in comparison to other
> people I know.
> I was only in Belgium for two days, the
> same in Poland. You don't necessarily
> have to have travelled a lot to know the
> world, I think.

You're right.
Do you want to travel more?

> I don't know. What doesn't interest me
> at all is a holiday in the classic sense.
> That's for people who can't otherwise
> escape their everyday lives.
> The theatre is enough for me; on stage,
> I can be anywhere I can imagine, I can
> be anything, a traveller, a spirit, an old
> man, an alien.

But what do you do when you're not on stage?

> Sleep.
> *Smiley*

★ ★ ★

She ordered a few books.

   Nigeria: What Everyone Needs to Know by John Campbell
and Matthew T. Page.

Chimamanda Ngozi Adichie: *Purple Hibiscus.*

E. C. Onsondu: *This House is Not for Sale* (Juno googled the book, it was about spirits, myths, mythical creatures, life in a working-class neighbourhood in a large Nigerian city).

Sebastian Conrad: *German Colonialism: A Short History.*

She didn't tell Benu anything about the books. She also didn't tell Jupiter. She carried them into her empty room when she came home from the bookshop and stacked them on the floor in a corner under the window.

Jupiter never came into this room; it had once been the living room. They had two and a half bedrooms, kitchen, bathroom. Because Jupiter slept so poorly and often had cramps and muscle spasms in the middle of the night, Juno moved into the half-bedroom to sleep at some point. The old living room with the planets was used less and less, so Juno had cleared it out.

When had Jupiter last been in there? She couldn't even remember.

She still didn't tell Jupiter anything about the chats with Benu. What should she say? At night, I chat with a stranger. Jupiter would probably tell her that she was very naïve.

That it was dangerous. With a stranger. Who knows what they'll do with your data.

What Jupiter wouldn't say: that Juno chatted extensively with a stranger but often exchanged only a few quick sentences with him. Because she had to leave again.

To go shopping. To rehearsals, to dance.

He wouldn't say that. He wouldn't even think that. But he would feel it.

FIVE

Juno, can you help me for a moment?

Jupiter was already in his wheelchair, dressed and ready to go, but only wearing socks. He couldn't get his shoes on.

Of course, said Juno, let me help you.

They wanted to go to Berlin. Jupiter was in the final round of a big literary competition. He had written a novel, and now he and five other authors would read from their manuscripts in front of an audience. At the end, a prize would be awarded for the best work. They had to get to the train.

Juno only knew about the literary world through Jupiter. Sometimes, she accompanied him to readings or to the Leipzig Book Fair, where she saw primarily earnest, somewhat stiff people in jackets and calf-length skirts, who drank a lot and became ever more high-spirited and talked louder as the hour got late. Before the pandemic, there were always glittering parties before the Leipzig Book Fair. Earlier, when Jupiter was still healthy, they had often gone, and Juno had watched the uncoordinated people from the literature world dancing, something that gave her a voyeuristic thrill. And that to such good music.

The main thing was that they were having fun, said Jupiter, when they were at a party like that for the first time, and Jupiter laughed.

Juno wanted Jupiter to win the prize. For the joy. For his health. For the money.

It took a while before Jupiter's feet slid into the shoes. Jupi's right leg could hardly move; he had no muscle control; his knee did not bend. You had to push the shoe firmly and steadily over his foot.

A little later, Juno heaved Jupiter in his wheelchair onto the tram. Their new neighbour from the apartment across the hall had carried the heavy electric wheelchair down the eight steps from the front door to the street. Ridiculous eight steps.

As usual, all the passengers stared at her and Jupiter as they got on the tram, and as usual, she stared grimly back until the people looked away.

What did the people who looked at them this way actually think? Juno never came up with an answer to this question.

At some point, they were in the main train station, on platform eleven, where the ICE to Berlin was supposed to depart soon. Platform section E, outside the train station hall; they were waiting for the wheelchair lift. That big silver box with a foot-operated hydraulic pump. Antediluvian, as if from the times when you had to pump up air mattresses by stepping on a bellows.

Nobody was around to bring the silver box.

Seven minutes until departure.

Three minutes. And still no silver box in sight.

The train arrived. Juno felt the wind in her face. People bunched up at the doors of the ICE.

Something small and pounding and cold under Juno's collarbone. On the outside, she tried to remain calm, calm, calm. Then she shot the people streaming in the other direction grim glances, although they couldn't help her, Juno knew that.

But it was so hard to channel anger.

Do you know how it is when you're always reliant on the help of other people, who either never show up or always come too late? Even though Jupi has to plan every step out in the world days in advance?

Jupiter always had to be extra punctual. The wheelchair lift for the ICE had to be ordered five days in advance. They even got up an hour earlier than necessary, just in case anything went wrong. Jupiter might not get from his bed into the wheelchair fast enough. The neighbour who helps with the wheelchair might suddenly not be at home after all. Those sorts of things.

And that's not fair, cried Juno, silently, of course, but some people looked at them guiltily nevertheless.

There was a conductor up at the front. Juno hurried towards him resolutely.

The train has to wait! The wheelchair lift isn't here! This time, she really screamed; it echoed across the tracks.

Later on, she remembered that she stamped her foot and said something rude to a woman who rushed by her in a panic to one of the doors of the train.

And there, for a moment, the main station stood still. Juno had simply stopped it. You could hear the sparrows fighting over a few crumbs. Jupiter, where was Jupiter? He had rolled a little way off and was holding his phone to his ear.

He called the Deutsche Bahn's mobility centre, but no one answered, he said later.

Whistling in her ear.

A lifetime passed until the person with the clanking wheelchair lift rushed up.

Juno waited outside as Jupiter was lifted up to the door of the ICE with the wheelchair lift and rolled into the carriage. She saw the outlines of a few people in the windows, craning their necks, looking outside to see what was going on.

The train left with a ten-minute delay.

On the train, the first thing she saw was a sign on the disabled bathroom: Out of Service.

★ ★ ★

And why aren't you married?

> I like living by myself, I don't want a permanent relationship.

But aren't you lonely?

> No, not at all.
> I meet a lot of people, I go out in the evenings, drink a beer in the bar.

(Of course that was a lie.)

A woman shouldn't go to bars alone and drink.

> Why not?

No one can protect you.
It can be dangerous.

> I'm already much too old for someone to put something in my beer.
> And nobody would dare to do that to me anyway. I look such that stupid guys know not to tangle with me.

I wouldn't say that.

Juno felt flattered again but regretted it right away.

In any case, she was Juno Isabella Flock.

She was made of concrete. Had a heart of stone.

She also couldn't be fooled easily.

The little LED light that plugged directly into the outlet threw a glimmer into the room. She had moved everything away that could reveal too much about her; her phone's camera only showed her face. Her forehead shone and reflected the light back into the room; you could see the walls, a little bit of curtain.

For a few weeks, they had been talking to each other on video calls.

Another limit overstepped, Juno didn't forbid it.

All love scammers asked the women they were chatting with to get on a video call with them at some point. They used deep-fake technology for this; Juno had learned that in the love scamming documentary. The images from the fake profile were superimposed on the real scammer's body, so that when they spoke, you saw a white, grey-haired man in a chic shirt who was sitting on the sofa in his dentist practice or at home. It was high-tech but apparently working better all the time. There were instructions for this on YouTube.

But Benu was here as himself. He lit a joint, let the smoke rise, laughed, his eyes relaxed, or perhaps they always had been.

Error, error, error.

How could she be so naïve?

But there were no discoveries without naïvety. Sometimes you had to be able to suppress the possibility of death; otherwise, you couldn't move forward, and you had to be a bit naïve for that.

The sailors who wanted to go to the end of the earth were naïve too.

What an evil thought, one that came to Juno much too fast.

Admittedly, she was curious. Thus far, things seemed okay. He had always been funny.

The first time, Benu gave her an on-camera tour of his room. The walls were hung with colourful, batiked cloths. It was much cosier than her room, which was bare and nevertheless chaotic; there were things lying all over the floor, socks and books, weights for her workouts, little notes to herself and ballet shoes, boom box, empty teacups.

At Benu's: everything was tidy and clean. There was nothing extra lying around. He looked friendly, and also older than thirty-two.

Both a little embarrassed, they grinned at each other like teenagers, said little, had no idea what you were supposed to say in a video call.

What kind of a meeting was this? What was its purpose?

Benu, more carefree than Juno, had to laugh at her face.

He said again, she looked like a troll or an elf.

And that she was small.

I'm five foot five, said Juno.

Then she didn't know what else she should say.

They talked a little about the weather. Juno turned her laptop towards the window so that Benu could see the night sky.

Now, in the middle of their laughing about Benu's nice little sentence, the room suddenly went dark. Juno was familiar with this already; at eleven, the light in Benu's apartment (or house, she had never seen it from the outside) went out when the generator switched off. You could only see Benu's face, lit by the light of the display; the rest – body, furniture – had disappeared.

Today, Benu lit a candle. He carefully held one hand in front of the lighter so that the flame didn't go out with the draught and placed the candle on a table in the middle of the room.

It flickered.

Laugh again.

Um, why?

Because I like it.

But I don't want to laugh right now.

But when Juno said that, she laughed. She didn't know why this image struck her: how Benu lit the candle.

Who was she actually talking to?

Someone who didn't have any power after eleven o'clock.

She stuck to the facts.

Why was there no power after eleven o'clock in this city in Nigeria?

Stupid question. Because the power grid was a catastrophe. But why was it a catastrophe?

Because they had power 24/7 here in Europe.

Because they had everything and wanted to have everything.

Nothing that Juno had around her – heat, food, work – hurt anyone anywhere else.

Shortly thereafter, Juno happened to read in the newspaper that there was a currency reform under way in Nigeria. Elections were coming up; the central bank and government wanted to take stocks of old cash off the market to prevent people from buying votes. There were supposed to be new banknotes, but nobody could get them. Too few in circulation; the little new money circulating was hoarded by the few who got it early. The old banknotes were no longer valid after 18 January; the government blocked all requests to extend the validity period. You could get new notes from illegal dealers for a fee. Only in larger shops in the bigger cities could you pay with a card. More than one third of the population did not have bank accounts.

In short, the situation was dramatic. Businesses had to close, hardly anyone could buy food, even if they had money in their accounts.

What's happening in your country? Juno typed this into her phone then told him about the article.

That's right, said Benu, he couldn't withdraw any money right now.

His mother's stocks of food were slowly being depleted.

He hadn't eaten breakfast today.

I'm sorry, wrote Juno.

In the photos, she had seen that he looked a little bit thin. Once he said that he thought he was too thin, so he intended to go to the gym soon and lift weights.

It's okay, said Benu now, and thank you.

He didn't ask her for money, it wouldn't do any good.

In the next few days, Juno avoided this topic.

She read Benu's sentences, considered whether there was anything in them that she was not hearing or seeing. The aura of the scammer. She didn't know what she should write.

★ ★ ★

She had ordered some other books at the bookshop, searching aimlessly and wildly on the internet, with cowardly curiosity, or was it just a sense of duty?

Why We Matter.
White Thinking.
The Lies That Bind.
The White Stain.
Black Skin, White Masks (from the 1960s, Juno ordered it from a second-hand bookshop).

Juno thought that maybe the books could reveal something to her. She carried them into her room and stacked them in a corner on the floorboards. Perhaps she would take the books over to Jupiter some day, lay them on the table next to his hospital bed and say, Do you know why I'm reading all of these?

Much later, in the future.

Now she lay on the floor, reading a few sentences each evening, in the same way that you might sip from a cup of hot tea.

The sentences didn't always stick with her right away, but apparently your memory can save information even if you've read it quickly. First, you survive without knowing, but you'd still be able to pull the knowledge out later.

Outside, the first blackbirds were singing, mornings and evenings.

Juno listened to the music that sounded like the melody that plays in the film when Melancholia is turning, or if Melancholia were an animal,
its quiet whimpering or snarling,
she listened to all of this, all of this
under the ceiling of her room, under the stucco.

Reading these books was work. They were not written so they were difficult to understand; on the contrary, and they were very interesting. But perhaps that was it: that they were only very interesting for Juno. She herself could decide whether she would let what was in the books into her head. In one of the books, she read that white people had the privilege not to concern themselves with racism.

> Hi, what are you doing right now?

>> Hi, I'm lying on the floor, reading interesting books, namely (*insert title here*).

> Lol

She and Benu hadn't written this, but that's what the chat would probably look like. The Lol a small, amused laugh, then an awkward silence.

Once upon a time, Juno had thought that *Lol* was the abbreviation for *Lots of love*.

* * *

Now she and Jupiter had a little money; it would be enough to last six months. Because Jupiter won the literature competition. A crazy bolt from the blue, sudden and unexpected. He had read aloud, an excerpt from a novel that he had been writing for a few months. Juno hadn't heard much about it. Jupiter had only ever told her in passing that he was writing something. After Jupiter's last sentence, there was silence in the room, as if everything stopped for a moment, even thoughts, before the wave of applause broke, thick and palpable, like a monster wave; like something that people couldn't actually control.

The whole event took place in an old villa at the edge of Berlin, in a literature centre with creaky parquet floors and dark, wood-panelled walls. They entered the building using a lift that was in a side hall, and that an employee had to release with a key. A slightly ghostly silence reigned in the rooms, even if there were plenty of people in them. It was strange to fall suddenly into this silence, after the trip, the hectic scene with the wheelchair lift, the streets and trams that they had to be sure not to miss. Here, it was almost as if they were in a time warp.

The readings started a little later. It wasn't as pompous a competition as the one for the Ingeborg Bachmann Prize, which Jupiter always followed live online in June. Each time he sat in his wheelchair cursing for four days, shaking his head or somewhat placated. This competition was not transmitted live on television and on the radio; that's why far fewer people from the newspapers were there, Jupiter told Juno before the competition. It was quite relaxed. However, there was also money here, fifteen thousand euros. Fifteen thousand. The words sounded like a fanfare.

When it was Jupiter's turn to read, Juno rolled him up to the reading table in his wheelchair. You could see the thoughts of the people in the room rising like speech bubbles in comics.

Oh how brave. Oh how sad. Oh how great that she's come with him. Oh what an interesting couple. Oh what a burden. And a few more oh sentences. Juno had quite intentionally worn a close-fitting dress; she had pushed the sleeves up over her elbows so that you could see the tattoos on her forearms. And she was wearing eyeshadow in neon pink; it came from the music piece with Tristan and Phoebus. For the performances, she had applied the pink in generous wings around her eyes; it continued on to her temples and shimmered in the spotlight. This made Juno look like she had great big cat eyes.

Now it was more subdued, a slight neon swoosh on her lids, but visible enough.

The other authors sat at the front, in a row ahead of Juno. All of them were known quantities, Jupiter had told her. They rustled the pages of their manuscripts, and Juno saw and heard an author sitting directly in front of her shuffling his feet constantly, as if to make his impatience audible. But what kind of impatience was that? thought Juno. One that was directed at the situation; that is, at the fact that they were competing for fifteen thousand euros and had to endure nervousness and perhaps later humiliation – or was the man ungracious to the person who was sitting at the table and reading?

When the jury retreated to consult, there was a small lunch buffet, two large serving dishes of vegan vegetable stew and baskets with thick slices of bread. Juno was a bit disappointed; she was hungry, she'd only eaten a small breakfast in the morning, and she was hoping for an ample buffet. She took two bowls from a table and joined the queue; Jupiter stayed outside in the entrance hall. Juno had only been standing there for a minute when somebody tapped her on the shoulder from behind; it was an author who had also read. She was the last one to read. Juno liked her story, about a woman who, after a devastating natural disaster, lived in a treehouse in the forest. An environmental dystopia, something dark about it, a little eerie. Perhaps because the story sounded very realistic.

I love your dress, said the author. Juno thanked her and told her that the dress was very inexpensive; she'd bought it at a charity shop. Then there was a pause; neither one of them seemed to know what to say next. The woman was approximately Juno's age. Her hair was cut just over her shoulders in an irregular pageboy cut, Juno could see right away that she cut it herself. She always cut her own hair too; in time, you developed an eye for it. The queue in front of them moved forward, there was a gap between Juno and the person in front of her. The author looked a bit sorrowfully at the serving dishes. Are you excited? asked Juno. About the prize? Oh no, said the woman, I've long since stopped being excited.

Juno didn't dare to ask why.

As if the woman had read her thoughts, she said: It's not worthwhile getting excited about such prizes. I've never won one; meanwhile, I don't care. In the end, we all die, with or without prizes.

Then they looked at the serving dishes again.

I just hope that there's enough stew left for us.

At precisely that moment, four young people brought two new serving dishes in and replaced the ones on the buffet.

Perfect, said the woman.

Maybe that's a good sign, said Juno. Perhaps you'll win the prize.

The woman laughed.

And what do you do? she asked. Are you also a writer?

Now Juno laughed.

God forbid! she said.

Then came the usual embarrassment. What should she say about her profession? If you say you're a performance artist, you frequently get fantastical answers. Performance, that's what people call standing naked in a museum, isn't it?

A little something with theatre, said Juno to the woman; and that was right.

Great, said the woman. I also like theatre.

They had reached the serving dishes. Juno nodded to the woman. See you later, she said. And good luck!

She didn't know whether she really wanted to wish the woman luck. She wanted Jupiter to win. She filled both bowls and carried them to Jupiter out in the hall. They ate the stew right there, Juno standing and Jupiter in his wheelchair, balancing his bowl on his knees. They had been told a while ago that there would be a longer break. Two men, journalists perhaps, approached Jupiter and began talking to him. They didn't notice Juno at all, which suited her fine. She took Jupiter's empty bowl and carried it back into the room with the buffet; the queue in front of the buffet had dissipated.

A glass door led out to the garden. Juno pressed the latch, it was open.

A big garden. Tall trees, holding their bare branches in the wind and waving gently. There was a pond towards the back, not such a small one; there were coots bobbing on the water. Juno approached; perhaps she could take a picture and send it to Benu. Sometimes she had these impulses to give him small, quick insights into her environment, landscapes, streets, cities, rooms.

A sharp, peppery winter aroma hung in the air.

Juno approached the bank of the pond. She discovered a dead bird in the shallow water at her feet. Not a coot, but something small, larger than a blackbird. It was mud-coloured, that might have come from the pond's sediment. The bird lay there as if asleep yet completely lost and in the wrong place. Not a motif that she would send to Benu or anyone else. Nevertheless, she took out her phone.

In her photo app, she had a collection of pictures of dead but externally unscathed animals. A starling with dark, colourful feathers in the courtyard behind her building. A dove in the alluvial forest, a little off the path. A rigid garden spider on the windowsill in the bathroom. Even a wild duck, which lay unscathed and still splendid on the pavement at a cross-roads next to a bin. It was a somewhat unusual collection, but Juno had heard several people say that they had something like it, so it was okay. Perhaps many people liked photos like this because they were free of all irony and kitschy feelings. They were full of reality.

Juno went a little closer to the water. Still closer. Still closer. And then she lost her balance, something that didn't happen often.

Luckily the water near the bank was shallow, not even ankle-deep.

She landed with one foot right next to the bird and felt the water's cold straight away.

She turned to the terrace, Jupiter was there, the two men from before to the left and right next to him; they must have carried Jupiter and his wheelchair out, for the doors to the garden had a high threshold. They were smoking.

Juno waved. One foot in the water. Jupiter was far away. He waved back; Juno was not sure whether he saw that she was standing with one foot in the pond. And that wasn't important. In that moment, Juno was sure that Jupiter would win the prize. She imagined how she would roll him forward to the podium with a wet, squeaky shoe, and how he would get a bouquet of flowers and a few handshakes there.

And so it was.

It was actually the best moment of the day, thought Juno later. Her shoe had left a few shiny prints on the parquet floor.

When a man from the jury spoke Jupiter's name into the room, after a brief pause, the author from the buffet line turned to Juno and held up her hand. They gave each other a high-five.

SIX

All she saw were red dots on her messenger apps.

WhatsApp (2)

Telegram (4)

Facebook Messenger (1)

Gmail (2)

The two messages on WhatsApp were from Benu.

What are you doing right now? he'd probably ask.

Juno wanted to answer later.

Nothing special.

At that moment, she was watching a documentary, which, in a certain sense, applied to him as well.

The documentary was on Spiegel TV, about women in Germany betrayed by love scammers. They were all older than Juno, most of them over sixty, either widowed or divorced. Their rooms were full of wall units and three-piece suites, curtains hanging in front of the windows. A cosmos full of strange, sad pictures. And always only one lonely woman there.

One of the women took her own life, in her early sixties.

Her best friend visited her grave; the film began with a zoom-in on her gravestone. There she lay.

Her house was mortgaged, she had lost her job. She had sent more than 250,000 euros to the love scammer because he promised to come to Germany soon, her friend said.

They wanted to marry; he raved to her about their joint future and talked about a wedding. A romantic, white wedding after chatting for a year.

The woman's friend continued her report. All of a sudden, there was trouble with the supposed lover. His bank account was blocked, he was desperate, he couldn't access his money, but he had to plan the trip to Germany. He told her he needed a lawyer, said the woman's friend. He needed short-term financial help. Customs, a visa, doctors' fees, a new car for Europe. The woman paid. The love scammer told her that of course she'd get it all back when the situation with his account was cleared up. And so things continued; he had to go to the authorities, to the notary, then at last he needed the money for the flight. So he said.

Benu wrote again.

Juno saw the message light up on her lock screen; it indicated that he'd sent a photo.

Juno could not see the photo. To do that, she would have to open WhatsApp. She put her phone away.

The man had a car accident, so the documentary continued. One arm and both legs in plaster; he flashed a victory sign from his hospital bed (the documentary showed a photo that he sent the woman). He still didn't have access to his account; he had to pay the clinic, there were bank fees to solve the riddle of the blocked account. The woman kept transferring money, she paid and paid.

Another message from Benu.

How do you like that?

The question probably referred to the photo that he had sent.

She would look at it later.

As usual, Juno did some stretches; this actually felt a bit irreverent. She bent her upper body to the floor, pressed her breastbone on the floorboards. No sofa. No wall unit.

She had to think about the woman in the documentary, the one who was no longer alive. Perhaps she had stood at the airport gate with excitement. Soon her future husband would stand before her, a grey-haired, white consultant with a blocked account. He would set aside his rolling suitcase, take her into his arms. Pull a rose out of his sleeve or a ring from the pocket of his suit.

Things that most women had learned to imagine when they were thinking about *love*.

Unfamiliar faces streamed out of the gate.

There was nobody who looked like *him*, her white, grey-haired screen lover, with a few buttons open at his collar, sunglasses over his forehead.

People rushed by; everyone seemed to know exactly where they were going, everyone had a destination.

At some point, the woman must have understood that the world around her was real and mundane. Airport desks, conveyor belts, duty-free shops, people with hand luggage, real people in a real airport, but she was outside of it all, in a wilderness where there was nothing, not even a street, a house, a noise.

After that day, the woman couldn't find her way through reality, said her friend. The friend was filmed watering the flowers on the grave with a green watering can.

The scammer had deleted his profile that same day.

The woman had sometimes found the whole thing a little

strange, said her friend; she frequently didn't have a good gut feeling, but she believed in the good, hoped for the good. Hope, this evil superpower.

Then it became clear: she was just a machine that spat out euros, that was her only purpose.

And now she had been pumped dry.

Bam.

Claire, in *Melancholia*, did not open herself up to the certainty that the planet would hit the Earth.

She saw calculations of its orbit on the internet. It seemed that no rescue was possible.

But Claire wanted to believe John, her husband. John had bought a telescope and set it up joyfully in the garden, a hobby telescope, medium-sized, ambitious, but not necessarily useful for certainty.

John said that Melancholia was on its way back to outer space. When he himself no longer believed what he had said, he took some pills and went to sleep for ever.

Claire found him in the stall with the horses.

Claire: I'm afraid of that stupid planet.
John: It won't hit us.
Claire: Do you promise?

Older woman: You're real, aren't you, scammer?
Scammer: Yes, of course.
Older woman: Do you promise?

When she had finished stretching, Juno reached for her phone, opened WhatsApp. Benu's photo was a graphic, digitally drawn.

It was all in shades of green. Juno saw a figure, half human, half cloud, a kind of spirit or genie without a bottle that was rising up from the floor.

This genie had a giant joint in its mouth and looked amused.

Ha ha, funny.

Crying/laughing smiley
I drew that.

Cool.
Smiley

It was cold in the room. Juno had forgotten to turn the heat back on after airing out the apartment. She didn't know whether she really liked the genie. Whether the joint required so much attention. Or what the graphic was supposed to express. Perhaps it wasn't trying to express anything at all.

Is that a genie?

Or maybe the smoke from the grass.

Oh yes, that's right.
I like everything that has to do with ghosts.
Smiley

So, do you believe in spirits?

Not in real life, of course, but I think the idea is nice.
And then there was something strange.
When my father was terminally ill and it was clear that he didn't have much more

time, my mother's friends convinced her
to bring in a spirit healer.
Where I'm from, all the older people go
to the spirit healer when they're sick.
They also go to doctors, but not just to
doctors.
Even some doctors send people to
the spirit healer. The spirit healers are
always women.

And did your father get better?

No, unfortunately not. But he was
very quiet after the spirit healer did
something for him. That's what my
mother told me.

What did she do?

I have no idea. Nobody knows.
The spirit healer didn't want to see my
father in person, he was already in the
hospital.
She only wanted to go into the apartment.
In any case, my father suddenly got
very quiet, said my mother. Before that,
he was in a lot of pain. He died that
night.
My mother said that he went to sleep
peacefully and wasn't afraid at all.
I think about that sometimes. What that
was. It probably would have happened
that way even without the spirit healer.

But there's always that small bit of
uncertainty.

Perhaps it was only because your mother was with
your father. Her love helped him.

Yes, maybe that's it.

But then she wrote something else.
     Later on, Juno thought that she shouldn't have pursued
it, but then it was already too late.

I'd like to ask you something more
about the women, you know,
the scammer thing.

Longer pause.

I don't like talking about it.
I'm ashamed.

You don't have to be.
I'm just interested in the facts.

What do you mean?
I can't say very much about it.

Okay. Then sorry.
It's not important.

Other things are important.
Smiley

What have you eaten today?

An apple, bread and cheese, a tomato,
salad in the evening.

What have you thought about today?

I don't know any more.
Or rather, I don't know what
was so important that I should
remember it.

I thought about you.
That I wanted to send you the picture.

Oh.

Juno wrote something else like, More tomorrow, good night.
Then she put her phone down.

★ ★ ★

In the next few days, Benu sent more pictures of creatures
made of smoke who were smoking joints.
    It will be a series, he wrote.
    Some creatures stood on one leg, the only one they had. One
grew out of a big plant that looked like a sundew. Juno didn't
know if sundews grew in Nigeria. Another one lay coiled up in
the corner of a room; it had four hands. In one hand, it held up
the joint and lit it on a sun that was hanging from the ceiling.

I'm thinking about whether I should make more
of these and print them out.

Sure, why not?
Do you want to sell them?

Maybe, we'll see.

He had a lot of plans, perhaps that was normal at his age. One time, Benu wanted to open a shop to sell jeans; another time, an online store for perfume. He sent Juno pictures of bottles that he wanted to buy and then sell for twice as much, curvy bottles with gold caps and labels bearing names such as *Misty Love* or *Gold Dust*. In the meantime, Juno knew that this was one of the most common tricks of love scammers who had been exposed. They maintained contact with the women and pledged improvement. They wanted to open a business, find something to do in the future so they wouldn't have to scam any longer.

It just took start-up capital.

Benu didn't say anything about start-up capital.

Perhaps he had taken her far enough already that she would ask of her own accord.

Do you need money? Can I help you?

Sometimes Juno asked herself whether she would offer Benu money if she had thirty thousand euros in her account.

But if so, how much? Fifteen euros? Or a thousand?

She had never cared about money, and not because she had a lot of it.

As an artist, first you need talent; Juno thought such slogans were ridiculous.

The only prerequisite was that you could live on porridge for a long time and not think this was a bad thing.

Then she thought about how patronizing these thoughts were. The thing about oats wasn't such a special characteristic if it was clear that in case of emergency, you wouldn't starve.

★ ★ ★

I'm going shopping, do you want anything in particular? Jupiter lay in bed; he had stuck a reading lamp on his computer that illuminated his face from below. He turned his head towards her; he looked transparent despite the impenetrable fog around him, with his slightly reddened eye, the other one was hidden by a strand of hair. Maybe chocolate, he said.

Anything else? Long pause.

Nothing else. Just anything. Whatever occurs to you.

Okay, said Juno. Juno knew that she wouldn't think of anything. She wouldn't think of anything that she could buy. What a strange determination, but this was actually a not-insignificant part of her life: gliding without ideas through the aisles of the supermarket. Zombie Juno Isabella Flock wandering along the shelves, grabbing something, something that she assumed would be edible.

When shopping, she caught herself looking for older women, one here and one there and another one there. And there was another one over by the ready-made cakes. One was heavily made up and dressed in colourful clothes, the other three were sooner invisible, they wore muted colours.

Juno pushed her shopping trolley past one of the older women.

They were hardly ten years older than she was. She stopped in front of the freezer cases with the glass doors, her face mirrored in a panel. An oval smiley; the corners of her mouth were struggling not to turn down.

In secret, she thought how dumb the women were who fell for the love scammers.

Hello, my sunshine, how are you?

Women had learned that that's something nice.

Nice: flowers and compliments.

Nice: *I love you.*

★

At the cash register, the sleeve of her jacket slid up her arm a bit, when she was moving her items from the shopping trolley to the belt, and the tattoo on her lower right arm became visible. It was lettering: 'euphoria', floating letters made of double lines; there were four small butterflies flying around the word. Over it, a small deer; it looked like the one from the *Bambi* film.

The hands of the woman at the cash register were tattooed up to the fingers, and her neck was covered with drawings and patterns almost up to her chin. The tattoos were already a bit older, their lines a little blurred, and the black had turned into the usual denim blue. The cashier's gaze fell on the lettering. Then their eyes met for a moment.

She hadn't had her tattoos for long; in November, she saw a flash sheet on Instagram, by a tattoo artist she followed. Previously, either she had not dared or back then, in the 1990s, the zig-zag patterns would have been too big for Juno's arms, she wouldn't have liked them.

But now, 'euphoria'. Lettering like an effervescent little river, perhaps the Vils River where she was born. Like a night without sleep. The little butterflies around the outside did the rest.

She wrote a DM to the tattoo artist.

He answered and wrote that he would be a guest at a tattoo studio in Berlin in two weeks. Juno took the ICE. She had also fallen in love with a peacock eye; it was made of many delicate lines, she wanted it on the inside of her lower left arm. She wanted to see the tattoos when she was dancing.

When she wiped a tear from her eyes.

When she raised her hand to wave to someone.

She told him how old she was right when she made her request. She didn't want to see any surprised looks when the tattoo artist opened the door.

Also, Juno was afraid that her skin was too old, that the tattoos would bleed, the lines would blur.

No worries, said the tattoo artist, that was only a problem with very old people and not on every part of the body.

In the studio, Juno climbed onto the table and raised her eyes to look at a little dent in the ceiling. The buzzing of the tattoo machine started. Then the needles came into contact with her body for the first time.

Many little pricks, like memories.

At some point, the tattoo artist said over the buzzing that her skin was as tight as a thirty-year-old's.

Two hours later, she climbed down from the table with a few grams of ink in her body. She looked at herself in the big mirror next to the door and held her arms next to her sides. They looked good. The tattoo artist took some photos with his phone to document his art and sent her up to the front.

They came out really great, he said, and Juno saw that he was really happy. She got a loyalty card; six more tattoos from him and the seventh one would be free.

She'd definitely be back, said Juno, before she went out onto the street. She would make good on that.

At home, she rolled up her sleeves and showed Jupiter the tattoos.

Wow, said Jupiter, and he told her he was a little jealous. He didn't know whether he would dare to do that because of the pain. It probably wouldn't be good for his illness. Perhaps the nerves would be even crazier after a tattoo, with all the pricks and the ink. And I hardly get out of the house at all; who would even see the tattoos? said Jupiter.

I would, said Juno.

* * *

And so the days passed. Shopping again, shopping as always.

In the bakery section, she pulled two blueberry muffins out of the box with her bare hands, and a saleswoman snapped at her that she should use the tongs.

Sorry, said Juno.

She bought a few little pizzas for Jupiter because he liked them. He hadn't seen the inside of the supermarket for ten years or more and didn't know what it looked like and which products were where; therefore, he had no idea what was there.

Don't forget the tongs, Juno.

Soon it would be spring, soon there would be strawberries. What else could she buy for Jupiter? What else would make him happy? There were no more big surprises. In the last two years, they have had money; that was especially thanks to the pandemic, the special grants and extra funds. Jupiter got a good sum for his novel, Juno several grants from performing arts funds and, in the last year, a very well-endowed grant from the Berlin Academy of Arts for the music piece. Phoebus and Tristan got it too. In addition, she always led a few workshops, she even taught at the Giebichenstein Castle in Halle; interest in performance art and time-based media had increased noticeably. The sums were not large, but with the other money it amounted to a total that didn't decrease so fast. When she went shopping, she didn't always have to watch her pennies; sometimes at the supermarket she bought expensive lemonade, tiny bottles with beautiful labels for three euros, and last winter – when there was another lockdown and she couldn't perform in a choreographer's

piece but received some cancellation money nonetheless –
in that winter, out of sheer spite, she had bought imported
mangoes two or three times, five euros apiece.

But now the grants were gone. Meanwhile the money
taps had been turned off again and she and Jupiter were living
off the fifteen thousand euros from Jupiter's literature prize.

That was not so much more than two times the monthly
salary of high earners at the Deutsche Bank or Porsche, said
Jupiter once.

Sometimes Juno even cooked; kidney beans from the tin
with rice and carrots. Sometimes they only ate toast with
butter and cheese and a handful of cherry tomatoes for a
whole week.

When she made beans and rice, each time Juno left Jupiter
more than half in the pot, but Jupiter always took just exactly
half. Then each of them encouraged the other to finish what
was left in the pot. Jupi said: You need strength, and Juno said
the same to Jupiter. They didn't have to starve, but they were
always on alert.

About another twenty-three years, if everything went well.

* * *

A few hours later, in the middle of the night, when she was
chatting with Benu – they weren't talking about anything
in particular, just some of their usual small talk – Juno had
a sudden impulse to ask him what he had eaten for dinner.
She regretted the question immediately; perhaps it was naïve
and insensitive.

But Benu didn't think anything of it.

Fufu, a kind of porridge of plantains and yams, with roast
chicken and rice with vegetables. There was only chicken
when it wasn't too expensive and when you could get one at

the market. Actually, people only eat that on special days of the year, especially Christmas; then it was something really special. And the quantities were larger. But today his mother cooked it just because.

Benu wrote that he loved Christmas; good food, hanging around. But people drank too much outside. Did she drink alcohol?

> Not very often, I can only tolerate a little.

I never drink alcohol. Alcohol isn't good.
You shouldn't drink any either.

> No worries.
> *Winking smiley*

I really mean it. Alcohol is terrible stuff,
keep your hands off it.

> I only drink rarely, as I said,
> and when I do, a glass of champagne.

Stay away from it.
Promise me.
Emoji with folded hands

> What, why?
> I know what I'm doing, don't worry.
> *Smiley*

Benu responded that he hoped that was true.
Three days of silence followed.

* * *

Three days ago, a wild bee had moved into the insect hotel; since then, there was a constant soft buzzing on the window.

Juno wouldn't have noticed, but Jupiter asked her to be quiet when she came into his room.

He sat in his wheelchair, a little way from the window, and tilted his head.

That's a wild bee, he said, and listened.

Now Juno heard it too, a soft buzzing, which sometimes came very close to the window. Shortly after that, she saw a small body fly out of the insect hotel; it got lost in the air.

It's so early, said Juno, and Jupiter said that the insects were coming earlier because of global warming. Wild bees would fly early in the year.

The wild bee would make its nest in one of the hotel's holes and lay her eggs there. Then soon they would have a swarm of wild bees.

Jupiter often left his window open now, sometimes even at night; he said he was warm enough. His room led out to the balcony, in front of which stood a tall, old spruce. You got the feeling you were living in the middle of the forest.

Sometimes, giant spiders also got into the apartment; perhaps they were the Nosferatu spiders of which it was said there were more and more in Germany. A very big spider, previously only found in southern Europe.

In the autumn, Juno carried several giant spiders out of the apartment. Once upon a time, Jupiter had done that, when he could still take a few steps without the walker and he could stand for a few moments.

At first, when Jupiter couldn't do that any more, Juno rang Dorian's doorbell. He lived on the second floor and was tall enough that he could almost grab the spiders from the ceiling with his hand. But Dorian moved out, and for the last year a woman had lived in that apartment whom Juno didn't know well enough to ask. She had forced herself to sweep the spiders off the ceiling with a broom and put a glass over them after they fell to the floor. Meanwhile, she had learned how to shove a sheet of paper underneath the glass and carry the glass with the spider under it to the courtyard. The first time she did it she had heart palpitations, but by now she was used to it.

Now the wild bee had come. Juno stood in the middle of the room and didn't dare to move.

There it was again, the buzzing. She listened.

Juno saw that Jupiter listened like someone listening to music, with his eyes closed and a slight smile.

Quietly, she left the room.

She went down the long hall to the bathroom, and at first she didn't know what she was doing there. It was the room in the apartment that was furthest away from Jupiter's room.

She sat on the edge of the bathtub and cried.

* * *

The rehearsals for the guest performances in Munich started. They wanted to rework a few scenes and met every morning in a studio they had rented in an industrial area at the edge of the city. There was a small gallery there, and Juno felt like her tattoos were beaming towards it, as if they were small, special headlights.

Soon, people would be sitting in that gallery and they would see the tattoos. Juno had found a sleeveless top that she would wear underneath the spangled jacket. She would take the jacket off at a particular point in the performance.

The tattoos were the most special costume that she had ever worn.

Cool, said Phoebus, and laughed; he had a sleeve, his whole right arm was covered with a pattern.

And I will get more tattoos, said Juno, and Phoebus had to grin.

Perhaps people will think the tattoos aren't real, said Ariadne the next day. She was a performance artist who was a friend and who was watching the rehearsals. She said it admiringly, and at first Juno didn't know what Ariadne meant. After a few seconds, it became clear.

No one could imagine that the tattoos were real. Because Juno was too old for that.

And yet she would die with these tattoos, like everyone else with tattoos.

She sent Benu photos of the tattoos, and Benu sent her photos of his; he had two. A geometric, circular pattern on his upper left arm, delicate, like braided grass. A small star on his right hand, between his index finger and thumb.

Self-made, the star.
Laughing-crying smiley
Nice, your tattoos!

Thank you, yours too!

Do you want to get more?

Absolutely!
Perhaps stars, or the word Melancholia,
Planet emoji
Only something beautiful that I see. You just need to keep your eyes open, then you'll find something.

I tell myself this often, but I merely say it.

You think too much.
Negative energy, not good.
And remember, don't drink alcohol, okay?

What is it about you and alcohol?
You smoke grass.

But that's completely different,
You can't compare that.
Grass is medicine, something positive.
Alcohol is bad energy, devilish, please don't touch it.

Now I'm starting to feel like an alcoholic
when you write like that.
Emoji with two champagne flutes

I just want to look out for you.

You don't have to do that.
Smiley with a halo
Don't worry.

Don't joke about it.

Okay.

Look out when you go out.
You'll burn yourself, my impression.

(Somehow, he was right.)

Yes, I'll look out, I promise.
I don't go out very much any more.
I won't burn myself.

(I don't want to burn myself any more.)

Meanwhile, Juno regretted that she had lied to Benu so much in their first chats. That she always had a new guy. That she lingered in the theatre cafeteria for a long time in the evening. It was an image of herself that she didn't like, but one that she had found appealing.

A kind of counter-image, but to what exactly?

Now she didn't want to keep spinning this image out. She'd rather say normal things, something that was true. Something real.

> Did you know that there's now a wild bee living on my balcony? Are there any of those where you are?
> I think they're great, the loner among the bees, I like that.

At my aunt's house there are bees in the garden, yellow and fat, you have to watch out because they'll sting you fast.

> Perhaps living in a swarm makes you aggressive.
> Or having to work so much.
> *Smiley*

Laughing smiley

Bee emoji

SEVEN

There are events in the world that can be calculated in advance, such as solar eclipses or when asteroids and comets will fly past the Earth. And there are some that cannot be calculated in advance, such as solar storms. You can only record them and then determine reasonably precisely when the effects of the storm will hit Earth. The flare, the X-ray beam, takes eight minutes to reach the Earth. The plasma cloud requires two days.

These effects are not strong enough to disturb sleep. But who knows for sure?

Perhaps it was in the stars. In approximately two hundred days, it would be autumn again; they would have travelled another half journey around the sun. The wild bees of this Earth would have formed at least one new generation, and Orion would surely be there again, peeking up for the first time from his summer sleep.

Juno would stand between the shelves of the supermarket; this was a small, nasty certainty that she had to confront. She would take a package of 1.49-euro store-brand spiced Christmas biscuits from one of the promotional tables with the Christmas goodies.

In the middle of September, more precisely on 14 September, Juno would notice the date.

As always, the gingerbread, the domino cubes, the cinnamon stars and the spiced Christmas biscuits appeared in the stores in the middle of September. And everyone – just as always – got excited about this. Someone always cursed the incorrect timing.

On Instagram, there were thousands of photos of gingerbread stands in the stories. People wrote 'wtf???' or something about fucking capitalism.

But Jupiter was addicted to the spiced Christmas biscuits. His eyes lit up each time Juno brought the first packet into his room in September. She bought another one almost every day until December.

Because for a brief moment it made everything during the day easier.

Because she could make Jupiter happy and didn't have to think too much about how to do that. And she didn't care that it was still summer in Leipzig and that the people in the supermarket were wearing short dresses and short-sleeved shirts and Birkenstocks with no socks.

On this coming sunny 14 September, Juno would hear a younger woman she did not know, who looked much older than she actually was – for she was wearing glasses and a flowered dress and had a stern gaze – say to another younger woman next to her that the old people would start to buy their stupid Christmas goodies again. She would say that with the condescension of those who had only ever experienced good things in their lives.

That would happen in approximately two hundred days, Juno suspected this already, like you could predict the coming of a storm when the air was heavy, and the wind was blowing around many more leaves than usual. Juno also suspected how it would end.

With her, crying in the aisles of the Leipzig supermarket.

Where else in this supermarket could she reach, into which shelf, for which items? For more than fifteen years, she had been coming to this supermarket to shop for someone who could no longer do that for himself. Who for more than fifteen years asked her mostly for cheese, bread and pizzas. And for whom a packet of spiced Christmas biscuits in September was a real highlight. Juno wouldn't say all of this to the young, stern woman; she had already decided that. The woman wouldn't understand anyhow.

Perhaps everything that was supposed to happen in those two hundred days was just preparation for that 14 September.

Benu would be gone by then. She also suspected that.

Benu. A satellite that had got lost.

A wasp still lay on the windowsill in the dance studio; its body remained from last summer.

Juno took it home and took a picture for her collection before she put it into an empty matchbox. She put the matchbox on her desk; she didn't know where else to put it.

She was dancing as much as before the pandemic, sometimes in the evenings it even made her tired. Her abdominal muscles were still good; she had a small six-pack. And her calves were super; you could clearly see the two-part calf muscle; and her arms had always been long and beautiful.

On her back, you could see the latissimus dorsi and the little muscles arranged like waving fern leaves along her vertebrae. The autochthonous back muscles that keep the body upright, always up, up, the thing that distinguishes us from the animals.

Sometimes Juno thought that she had a beautiful body and that it was too bad that she could no longer show off this body in a club. For a women older than her mid-forties, it was no longer possible to dance through the night without being noticed.

Either you were a mascot that the younger people found 'cool' or you were a lonely old woman who wanted to hook up with someone for one night. You would have to be able to cope with all of this; only a few people could do that. Juno could not. She could only stand being noticed, if at all, on the stage.

* * *

It was a bad phase again. Or – what's actually bad? Other people might have called it that. Perhaps it was better to call it an exhausting-euphoric phase.

Juno slept a maximum of three hours, from approximately 4 to 7 a.m. Dreamless yet sensitive sleep, lurking, a little bit irritated. Then she forced herself to get up because she wanted to dance. First, she made coffee for Jupiter and put it in a thermos so that it stayed hot, because Jupiter often slept until 10 a.m.

Such routines were bleak but practical, a kind of support, as the walker was a support for Jupiter. The messages she wrote to Benu got out of hand, but that didn't seem to bother him.

> Sometimes I ask myself why it's a planet in *Melancholia* that crashes into the Earth, not an asteroid.
> But perhaps it doesn't matter for the film.

Hmm. I haven't been able to watch the film yet.

> In the end, Justine builds a little house of branches with Claire's son. Justine helps Claire into the little house.
> Claire hardly makes it in because she's nearly paralysed with fear.

But Justine is very calm.
Quite recently it was precisely the
other way around, Claire had to help
Justine into the bath, Justine could
hardly lift her feet.

Do you believe in God?
I believe in him.

Earlier I did, but no longer.
I believe in outer space.
I would like to be an astrophysicist.

Lol.
Red-exploding-star emoji

Benu sent a GIF too.
Jerry, the mouse from *Tom and Jerry*, splitting his sides
with laughter.
Juno didn't know if that was meant ironically.
She just sent a smiley back.
Then Benu sent the flames emoji.

You're a little crazy.
I like that.

Then, right away, the blue butterfly emoji.
Then the red buds emoji. The emoji with the radiant star.
And another emoji with the radiant star.
And another one.

Juno didn't know whether she liked that Benu liked that she
was a little crazy.

Or rather, that he wrote that he liked that.

Briefly, she had liked it. It was like falling from a very great height in a dream. In the first second, it was great. Then came the panic. Then you woke up.

* * *

The normality of everyday life had its good side as well. It was fragile, it suited the winter, which sometimes came and sometimes didn't. Normal life that was gruesome and full of secrets at the same time; you could dive into this everyday life and try to live intensively in it. And maybe sometimes you would succeed.

Just a few days ago, the health insurance assessors visited them. Someone came once a year to see whether Jupiter still needed help and hadn't, as if miraculously, suddenly been cured or healed by a faith healer.

Someone had to check whether there was still a reason for all the care.

Jupiter received a care allowance of a little more than five hundred euros.

For this, he had to have a score between 42.5 and 57 points on some scale. The points were for everything that Jupiter could no longer do by himself. If he couldn't go to the toilet, couldn't wash himself. Those scored the most points.

A woman had rung their doorbell and stepped into the hall. She was wearing glasses with a heavy rectangular frame and smiling in a manner that indicated that she didn't want to seem nice, but also not impolite.

In Jupiter's room, they sat on the chairs that Juno had set up for them.

The woman pulled a folder out of her bag, opened it and

began filling out a form, probably with the date and Jupiter's name.

Then she asked questions, hardly looking up from the form, and after each answer she made a quick, energetic check mark.

Whether Jupiter could wash by himself.

Whether Jupiter could make his own breakfast, lunch and dinner.

Whether Juno cooked for Jupiter.

Who put Jupiter's socks on.

Who put Jupiter's shoes on.

Who combed Jupiter's hair.

Who showered Jupiter.

Jupi and Juno told the truth, but they still lied.

If both of them had told only the truth, namely, for example, that Jupi usually put his socks on by himself because he didn't want Juno to help him, the woman would have deducted points.

It's all about the bigger picture, is how Juno wanted to answer each question.

Their little questions and our little answers don't reflect the picture at all.

Of course Jupiter can make coffee by himself, but what would happen if I weren't there all the time?

If Jupi had to make coffee by himself all the time and then wasn't able to do it as well because it exhausted him.

If, for example, the Earth would deviate just a fraction of an inch from its orbit, just briefly once, just a quick roll, do you know what would happen then?

If I weren't there, then a carer would have to come, and that costs twice the care allowance.

What counts is that I'm the safety net.

And that's worth something, you know.

Juno didn't say any of this out loud, but the woman looked up from the form anyway.

The whole time, she'd been looking at the paper, and wrinkles had formed around her chin. Juno had been looking at her the whole time.

And what kinds of things do you cook? asked the woman suddenly and looked right at Juno for the first time.

Juno didn't know what kind of a look that was, if it was friendly or icy, and she thought that she wasn't even sitting on the chair but rather floating slightly above the seat, her legs crossed in the lotus position.

She reeled off a series of dishes that she had cooked at some time. Earlier.

Vegetable risotto, potato casserole. A lot of salad and vegetables. The main thing is that it's healthy, said Juno. And that she and Jupiter were vegetarians.

You're both a bit on the thin side, said the woman. Do you cook large enough portions?

Pause.

That's just the way we are, said Juno. We are thin people. I actually think that's great.

The woman looked a bit baffled for a moment, then bent over the folder with the form again and signed it, slowly and carefully.

She said: Then we're all done, and closed the folder.

That everything was okay.

That nothing had changed.

That she wished both of them the best.

They said their goodbyes, and Juno walked the woman to the door.

Only then did she notice that the woman was wearing a swinging, calf-length pleated skirt, with special shoes.

The ones which, instead of having a normal cap at the front, look like toes.

The thick paws of a clumsy, affecting monster from a comic book.

When she went back to Jupiter in his room, she saw that a tear was rolling down his cheek.

Juno sat back down on the chair, and they were silent for a while. It was as if the woman from the insurance company were still there, a ghost. Then Jupiter said he would go into a nursing home later on.

No way! said Juno. This response shot out of her mouth like a lightning bolt.

When she remembered this conversation later, she thought how abominable it was to sustain its banality. The ugly pictures of an everyday world with words such as 'nursing home'.

How did Jupi think that would go? she asked.

Such a bleak sentence. How could they even imagine it?

As if from a TV series. Juno didn't like TV series, she always felt fooled.

For she would have to move into the nursing home too, and she couldn't see herself there.

Why? You don't have to. Jupiter seemed to really mean this.

Do you think I'll let you move into that hell alone? Juno didn't even have to say that out loud.

Jupi shouldn't think that she would remain by herself in the apartment and visit him each day in the nursing home.

That would be absurd. Such sentences. They sounded just awful.

Sentences unlike ones in the real world outside, where

there was music, song, birds tweeting, the crowing of a cockerel in the morning, and such things. Or the cry of a revolution, something that a lot of people would hear.

But these sentences lingered in their apartment and only Jupiter and Juno heard them.

The ghost of the health insurance woman sat on the other chair, looking from Jupi to Juno and back again.

As far as I'm concerned, we can move into a hotel, said Juno. Like the wild bee.

Jupiter said: Can't you talk to me about this seriously for once?

I am serious, said Juno. We'll just stay here. What could change so much from how things are now? Nothing will change. It will stay as it is.

She went into the kitchen and unloaded the dishwasher. Doing something, something with her hands, something that made noise, that chased the evil spirits from the apartment. And then they didn't talk about it any more.

* * *

And precisely now, in this euphoric phase of normality, when she once again couldn't fall asleep – when she slipped into the kitchen nearly every night, made herself a cup of tea, and sometimes discovered that between movements she kept standing there in front of her reflection in the balcony door – where she looked distorted, like a figure from a Francis Bacon painting, that wasn't her at all – precisely now, more Instagram messages were raining down on her.

No requests from love scammers.

Those came too, but Juno hardly ever responded to them.

Real people with real profiles were also writing to her,

people who had been following her for a while but whom she did not know personally.

Although she had long since reached the age when women disappear.

She had a public profile, one that seemed to attract or invite some people.

She had become a bit better known in Leipzig due to the music theatre piece, and this became a minor grass fire on Instagram, a brief mini-fame, which extended just beyond Leipzig and wouldn't last long, that much was clear.

Two or three people wrote from Leipzig, another from Frankfurt, one from Berlin.

They all wrote similar messages.

They told Juno she has a nice figure. What she's doing is so interesting.

One from Leipzig wrote that she is a great artist. He had seen her in a performance. Would Juno give him a call?

Another sent long, intricate voice messages that Juno did not understand. He was talking about pseudo-philosophical matters, and the messages often ended by telling her that the person who was sending all of this would soon be in Leipzig. Perhaps they could meet.

One sent her poems every now and then.

Sometimes Juno answered one or other of them.

She kept lying, just as she had lied to the scammers.

And sometimes it was fun.

My father was into theatre.

He was a hobby actor with the theatre group of the volunteer fire department in our village.

And your father?

As a child, I was allowed to live in a
treehouse in the garden in the summers,
we had a big garden.

I made small beds with radishes and
carrots.
It was great at night, you could hear the
hedgehogs spitting.
I knew that it was hedgehogs, but
pretended they were monsters.
What did you do as a child?

She wrote about what she imagined was a nice childhood.
Nothing about what she had done, not a topic she would
have chosen. It just happened by itself and she only noticed
when she sent the messages. Most of the people who wrote
to her weren't interested in her childhood, invented or not.
Some bowed out quickly, some stayed silent for a while only
to pop up again a few weeks later.

It was a small, sweet meanness to lie to these men.

Or a way to sneak out of these conversations without
having to be impolite.

This is what she had done with Pluto, a man with wildly
layered hair. He was about her age.

She had lied to him and noticed how in the process, a
nice feeling of malice spread through her, almost a form of
hatred, which she could discharge in a gentler way by lying.

Sometimes, she went to another dance studio, to a group
that danced contact improvisation. The people there wore
wide trousers and hugged each other long and hard when they

arrived. Sometimes, Juno liked to dance with this group. Contact improvisation was the opposite of ballet; you danced as you wanted to, touching the bodies of the others, hugging, lifting, pressing against the weight of another person.

If you didn't want to dance, you didn't have to; you could sprawl in a corner and daydream.

Most of the people were young, in any case younger than Juno. Besides her, there was only one older person, and that was Pluto. Pluto had asked her for her e-mail address on the very first evening in the studio. It was a kind of Christmas party, there were biscuits and mulled wine after dancing, and Pluto sat down next to her and asked her what she was doing. Pluto looked like someone who earned a lot of money. You could always see how rich or poor people were, especially men, thought Juno. When they earned a lot, they always had these tanned faces because they had time to take bicycle tours or go sailing. And they had big stomachs, even if they were otherwise thin, because they drank wine all the time.

Juno had been too polite to decline the question about her e-mail address; something that she later regretted.

When Pluto's e-mail came and he wrote that he was looking forward to dancing with her again, he asked what she did in her spare time. She responded that she never had any spare time.

Juno thought that would be clear enough.

But now, after dancing, when everyone was putting on their jackets and shoes, Pluto came and asked her what she was going to do today.

Juno said she had to go to the observatory in Schkeud-itz. I work there. She looked Pluto in the eye as she said that.

A few other people heard that too and turned around to look at them briefly. Slightly quizzical laughter. Pluto looked as if he didn't believe her, then he did, he looked at her with respect. Which turned right back into doubt.

Juno was tempted to relieve him of the burden, to end the game.

She wanted to say, I'm just kidding. But strictly speaking, she wasn't kidding but instead showing a little consideration. Sometimes people couldn't stomach the truth, and it was better to tell an obvious, unashamed lie.

All of the women, for example, who fell for the scammers, didn't want to see the truth even though they actually knew what they were doing.

Pluto also didn't want to know the truth, otherwise he wouldn't have asked her what she was doing that evening.

People didn't want to believe that they were mortal, but even before that, they didn't want to believe that they were lonely.

The love scammers didn't want to believe that they actually were making themselves look small and bowing to Western mechanisms of exploitation and greed because they bled people dry and threw them away. Furthermore, they were also mortal, despite the good profit that many of them were making.

Astrophysics, said Juno to Pluto. I'm directing a project that explores exoplanets.

In Schkeuditz. How Pluto put a small, confused emphasis on *Schkeuditz*.

The others around her were engrossed in tying their shoes or putting on their boots.

I'm only in Schkeuditz for mediation with schools. Juno articulated each individual word carefully. The subsidies we receive for our project are for knowledge transfer.

Another strange pause, in which everything in the world that didn't make sense was revealed.

Of course it was first and foremost Juno's meanness, a microaggression, and not a form of consideration.

On the way home, she stood on the Karlbrücke, took pictures with her phone.

The shimmering, dark band of the White Elster River, with the moon over it.

The camera no longer worked well; in the photo, a long ray of light ran diagonally through the orb. On the display, it looked as if it had just been hit by something else.

★ ★ ★

It was surprisingly nice to have a wild bee as a house pet.

A quiet, gentle, friendly guest. Sometimes Juno worried that the wild bee couldn't find enough nectar outside. At the end of February, it had been really warm and even sunny sometimes, a few tentative snowdrops were sprouting, the first pollen was also flying around, but maybe it wasn't enough?

And then the sky: Orion, who was only visible during the evening hours and disappeared later at night behind the western horizon.

Jupiter, which appeared directly over the moon, easy to find, you just had to look long enough, then you could see it. From the Industriestraße, for example, which connected two parts of the city with a bridge across the White Elster River.

Shall we have another video call? wrote Benu.

Okay, she typed into the speech bubble, I'll be home in ten minutes.

Then she walked in the other direction along the Industriestraße, slipped quietly into the apartment, this time it was dark behind the door to Jupiter's room.

She looked at her reflection in the windowpane.

It was okay as is.

She tried to make a neutral face.

Not to smile, if that was possible.

Hi, she said to Benu shortly thereafter, then smiled into the camera.

What's up with you?

They talked a while, Benu asked about the wild bee; Juno said the bee was doing well.

In the background, she heard several children laughing loudly and playing.

She didn't ask whose children they were.

It was his mother's birthday and the whole family was celebrating, said Benu, as if he could read her thoughts.

Should he take his phone into the kitchen?

I could introduce you to my family.

Oh, said Juno. I don't know.

They're crazy, you know, said Benu.

Juno saw that he raised his eyebrows and rolled his eyes as if he were playing, but he also seemed a bit serious.

You don't want to, do you? Benu smiled. No problem, it was just a thought.

Okay, said Juno, maybe next time.

They always spoke only at night when Jupiter was sleeping or watching TV or football. Sometimes, when Jupiter was up longer and went to the bathroom more frequently, they made a date for later, 3 a.m., and Juno set an alarm. Only in case she should fall asleep. She felt ridiculous and was ashamed of herself.

She told herself that her interest was artistic. Who knows

what talking to Benu might be good for. Perhaps for the theatre piece, which she wanted to start writing at last.

Nevertheless, everything about the chats and calls was actually wrong. A connection that was based solely on lies, or rather, on falsehood. And from the falsehood came exploitation. For in essence, it wasn't anything but that: she exploited Benu, and it didn't matter whether he was perhaps still trying to exploit her. One exploitation did not justify another.

★ ★ ★

Naturally the YouTube algorithm had continued to place additional documentaries in her list of suggestions. White, European women of middle to older age, who travelled alone or in groups to Gambia, Kenya, Thailand or Bali.

Juno saw how a man on a beach in Kenya tugged at the hand of an elderly white woman. They walked through the waves, then you saw them sitting at a table in a beach bar; they were drinking beer and eating something from small white plates. The woman was wearing a pink bathing suit, and you could see the wrinkly skin around her armpits and on her neck. She was much older than the man, who looked young. Definitely no older than early or mid-thirties.

The man said *I love you* to the woman and held her hand. He took her in his arms, kissed her forehead. The woman beamed and had a happy face.

And what if this was real? Juno wiped the thought away. First the man smiled, then he looked away from the camera.

Quite a few white, Western women took this kind of holiday every year, explained the documentary. The point wasn't a quick hook-up and to move on to someone else the next day as the European men did, the ones who flew to

Thailand or the Philippines and slept with an average of two women each day.

The women who flew to Ghana or Kenya had a boyfriend for two weeks. Sometimes they came back to him each year. They paid for his phone, the school fees for nieces and nephews; they bought him T-shirts, pizza, golden watches. It didn't seem to matter to them that they had to pay for so much.

Juno asked herself whether they had ever examined their bodies and faces and found themselves ugly.

It's good when the world ends, says Claire in *Melancholia*.

Tattoo across the back: White bitch.

Tattoo on the arm: Potato.

Juno wrote these sentences in her notebook, in a new file. Notes for something, perhaps for the theatre piece.

In the next few days, she looked away when a dark-skinned man passed her on the street. For the first time, it became clear to her what it meant to be ashamed on behalf of someone else's behaviour.

You just had to be wealthy enough, then you could travel to Kenya, Bali, Gambia and keep a lover boy. Pay for his pizza, give him a new phone.

Juno herself needed a new phone. The display soon gave up the ghost; small holes were burning from the inside of the device to the outside and forming little bubbles.

Note to the file:

Come to me, new phone, shimmering with rare earth from the soil of an African country.

Another note to the file:

Tattoo line (stolen from Ingeborg Bachmann):
Mankind can handle the truth.
I would most like to have this tattooed across my breasts.

★ ★ ★

Once, for several months, Juno also lived at someone else's expense. Achilles, whom she was dating at the time, had transferred a thousand Deutschmarks to her each month. That was when she had lived in Berlin for a few years; she had just turned twenty. She was dancing in smaller and sometimes larger productions in the freelance dance scene and hardly earning any money. In the mornings, she taught spinal strength and conditioning classes at the adult education centre.

At first it was nice not to have to teach the classes any more.

Juno didn't feel exploited by Achilles, although he was eleven years older; their relationship fitted perfectly into the usual scheme.

But Achilles was as generous to everyone in his circle of friends. It held no special meaning for Juno that he gave her money. He was always helping out his friends if they were having a hard time financially. Sometimes Juno heard about this. Often, he didn't want the money back. Juno didn't know why he had so much money, perhaps he had inherited it; she never asked. Achilles also never boasted about his wealth, he wasn't the type who treated everyone to champagne in bars or who drove a convertible. From the outside, you didn't even notice his wealth.

Juno didn't know why she was even dating Achilles. They actually didn't see each other that much.

Perhaps it was due solely to the thousand marks.

That's okay, said Achilles, when she mentioned it once.

You don't have to love me. There's no such thing anyway.

That's why he could take care of everything with money. If it wasn't associated with any expectation, it was truly pleasant. It simplified everything.

But what would you do if you suddenly didn't have any more money? Juno asked.

Achilles responded that this was a moot point. Nothing like that would happen. He didn't even have to think about it.

Juno ended the relationship, and so she was once again running back and forth across the city to the adult education courses. Spandau was Thursdays, Marienfelde Fridays, sport and play with people over fifty. Aqua aerobics in the indoor pool in Siemensstadt, always Mondays. In summer, she did laps on the track with the Siemens seniors. Everywhere in her courses and everywhere else, things were normal. People with shopping bags and raincoats. Gymnastic balls. A bakery with a counter at the Lichtenrade S-Bahn station. No craziness. Always the same times. People came regularly and on time to Juno's classes, they were friendly to her, and they were happy when she paid attention to them.

Normal life. Juno wanted this so much for herself.

Teaching the courses was much more normal than accepting a thousand Deutschmarks a month as a gift from Achilles.

In the end, the normality of the courses all around her didn't help any more.

More and more often, she was thinking about her place in the mountains, about the Vils River, that little river, how it bubbled down in the valley and was deep green. How she swam secretly there as a child in summer, below her an indescribable cold that reached all the way down to the tips of her toes.

How undisturbed and unobserved she was then.

Juno moved back to the mountains.

For three years, she worked in the only gym in town, at the desk, handing out keys for the lockers and pouring isotonic sports drinks for the guests. She had wanted to teach dance in the gym, but most people wanted to take classes where they could lose weight and get thin. Juno had ordered them around in crossfit bootcamps and forced them to do strenuous exercises. She was gruff and businesslike with them. But most people wanted to watch someone who was full of infectious zest for life, who put on a show for them.

Juno had played at this, but she didn't like the role. Then she found the magazine about Leipzig in the gym, in the quiet zone with couches, near the sauna. Leipzig, a city that looked like the Vils River. Green and a little bit enchanted.

A city where she knew no one, where she could be alone and unobserved.

There must also be a lot of adult education centres and gyms in Leipzig.

* * *

As expected, more snow fell. White, German snow. Snow that looked good at first, but did not stick around on the street.

Snow that again killed the carefree summer insects.

The wild bee was already dead by then. At some point, Juno had noticed that it wasn't flying around any more. No more buzzing to be heard from the balcony when she sat in Jupiter's room for a while.

Jupiter said it was long since dead.

It had been for about ten days.

Wild bees don't live very long, only about four weeks.

Juno was shocked; she had thought the bee would stay longer, perhaps as long as other house pets stay.

Will a new one come? she asked, and Jupiter said that the young wild bees had to come out of the eggs first.

But they will not stay, said Juno.

No, they will not stay. They will look for new hotels.

* * *

It also snowed suddenly in *Melancholia*; a winter began shortly before the impact. The prelude from Richard Wagner's *Tristan and Isolde* was heavily reworked for the *Melancholia* soundtrack; for example, there was no cello in the original. She still needed to listen to the prelude, out on the street when she was walking.

Juno was ashamed that she listened to Wagner, but she couldn't stop.

Eight p.m., everything was lit up, neon signs, the health food shop, subway, the bank.

She passed by a bar, people in it, young people that you could see through the big windows, they were laughing and gesturing; you could see them beaming and glowing. Still.

In sixty years, they would be a lot older than she was now. Sixty years, as good as nothing.

Nevertheless, they were only one-quarter on Earth.

She was this emoji with the dotted outline.

Once again, there was a letter to be posted. It was urgent, Juno was actually much too late on the draw. This time, the letter was from her to the Ministry of Culture. The accounts for the music theatre piece, the Ministry of Culture had already warned her, she couldn't wait any longer. There were several sheets in the envelope: the audience statistics; the final cost accounting; the list of payments; personnel and material costs; and the final report.

At the postbox, she pulled the envelope out of her bag,

there was a dark coffee stain on it. Maybe the paper inside had stains on it too. She could have downloaded a new form from the city's homepage and reprinted it, but then she would have had to fill it out anew. You could see the numbers on this form. Perhaps she would send an e-mail to the clerk tomorrow and explain everything.

The light piled up so high above the streets that nothing could soften it.

Many hours earlier, at about 9 a.m., Jupiter had a toothache.

Juno heard him through the panes of the glass doors. Leaning on his squeaky walker, he went into the bathroom and back into his room, swearing because there was no more ibuprofen.

Juno slipped into her trainers and hurried to the pharmacy. Meanwhile, Benu had written her.

Hey.

I don't have any time right now.

Okay, sorry.
Take care of yourself.

Yes, don't worry.

At home again, Jupi's pain was worse, the ibuprofen didn't do anything. He would probably have to go to the dentist, said Jupi.

It was about 10 a.m.; Juno had filled out the form for the final report and folded it up quickly. She put it in an envelope, it was already lying ready on her desk, and she left the letter for later. Okay, she said and got ready; she had to ring the doorbells of a couple of neighbours.

She didn't like ringing the neighbours' doorbells. Not because they did not generally want to help, but because each time there was this brief, surprised pause after they'd opened the door to Juno and said a jaunty, *Hello*.

Or the sobering of their gazes after they had opened the door with anticipation, in the belief that it would be someone else standing outside.

Jupiter's wheelchair weighed at least 50 kilos; unless she had help, she couldn't get it down the steps from the front door to the pavement. She needed a second person, and Jupiter also had to be supported as he moved down the steps. Sometimes he couldn't bend his right knee and put his foot on the next step.

It was one of the miracles of history that at least the neighbours in their building were friendly, and some were even at home during the day. Hippolyta from the first floor helped them; she carried the wheelchair down the steps by herself. She cleaned offices in the evenings and had strong arms. Jupiter fought his way down the steps on his stiff legs. On the last few steps, Juno put both her hands around his ankle and pulled his foot until the leg yielded and sank one step lower. Then finally Jupiter fell into the wheelchair that was already waiting for him on the pavement. The dentist's office was just down the road on the main street. There was a lift. Juno sat in the waiting room while Jupiter was being treated. She looked out of the window; the office was on the fourth floor. The sky was clear, that evening you would be able to see the constellations. Orion drawing his bow. Suddenly Juno thought of the story with Artemis, the goddess of the forest and the hunt, who killed Orion with an arrow without knowing it because Apollo told her that she should aim at the bright point far away over the sea. In her grief, she hung Orion as a constellation in the sky.

At home again, Juno had to ring another neighbour's doorbell, Hagen on the third floor, for Hippolyta had already left for work.

Everything worked out. At some point Jupiter was back in his room with a sealed tooth, without pain. There's nothing more to say about this.

That's all. It's everything other than a story from Greek mythology. Later on, Juno had to go out again, to buy toilet paper.

Later, she sat at her desk to start the theatre piece. Actually, she typed a few initial words on the keyboard, something that sounded like angry people who talked over each other, a chorus of the exploited (this is what she imagined); at first it didn't matter what kind of exploitation was at issue.

Later, she rehearsed her lines for the music piece with Phoebus and Tristan.

Later still, she did some dance exercises in her room, just a few, then drank a cup of coffee at her desk and moved a few items on the desk back and forth. She knocked the coffee cup over and spilled coffee on the items on the desk, also on the envelope for the Ministry of Culture; the coffee ran down the narrow left side of the envelope.

Juno quickly pulled the envelope away.

There was nothing more to say about this run-of-the-mill day, when Juno's level of peril and the general level of peril in Germany was nearly zero.

Compared to Benu's struggle with currency reform, the struggle with the letter was nothing at all.

But Jupi's toothache was a different story. The stress

with the wheelchair and the steps to the street were, strictly speaking, in this same category.

And the fact that something else had gone off course. That she had spilled the coffee because everything had started to sway.

By what measure can one tell whose story is less futile?

But who is threatened by death in the story and who isn't?

But when do you start being threatened by death?

★ ★ ★

Now, in the evening, on the street, she was not afraid.

Sleet, orange from the light, pattered on the ground; a snowstorm had blown in from the west in the afternoon; you couldn't see Orion. Nowhere a warrior with a bow.

Her phone rang. It was the pearly ring tone of the video call.

A video call outdoors, without WiFi, cost too much data.

Before she could see Benu on the display, Juno said exactly this into the phone: that the call would cost her too much data and she couldn't talk now. Nevertheless, she didn't hang up. The screen popped up, she could see Benu's face for a moment. Then the camera panned around a room that Juno had not seen before. A kind of kitchen, a shelf on the wall with bowls and jars of preserves, a table with a hob; on it stood an aluminium kettle. Somewhere there was a curtain made of beads or fringe.

Benu pushed his way into the picture. First, Juno saw only his forehead and eyes, then his whole face, and suddenly another face squeezed in, a man about Benu's age. He too was smiling, peering curiously into the camera. Now both of them were waving and Benu cried: Hi! How are you?

In the tiny thumbnail at the bottom, Juno saw herself; she looked a bit bewildered. Benu and the other man were laughing now, they seemed to find it funny that she was bewildered.

This is Feomi, said Benu. A friend.

Benu hugged Feomi and ruffled his hair. Feomi let him and laughed again.

Hi, said Juno, tried to wave.

She was walking along a street in Leipzig, it was snowing, and she was on a video call with two men in Nigeria, a call that cost a whole lot of data; and all this under the asterism of the Winter Hexagon, which nobody saw due to the weather conditions.

They talked about the weather. Juno held her phone in the light of a streetlamp; you could see the sleet, grainy, lit-up shadows, then she filmed a passing car, and a little bit of a nearby building.

Benu held his phone camera up to the window, where Juno could see a dark sky.

Do you see the stars? she asked.

Later, she remembered that she had asked them this.

Feomi laughed aloud; he wasn't used to questions like that.

It's cloudy, said Benu, no stars.

He said that with a touch of gentleness, as one might speak to an excited animal.

Juno no longer remembered how she answered.

In one of the documentaries about the lover boys, a young man sat in his family's living room. There were a few people around him, mother, aunts, siblings; the young man had passed a photo around.

His white lady.

The photo passed through everyone's hands. The man's younger siblings and his friends looked admiringly; his mother and a few aunts said something that Juno didn't understand; it wasn't translated in the documentary. The mother hugged her son and kissed him on the cheek.

Nobody seemed to find things strange with the white lady. In some families, people were even happy when a son had a white lady, the documentary explained. It was like having a good job.

Juno asked herself if the documentary was actually serious journalism.

She remembered how Benu wanted to introduce her to his mother recently.

And now his friend Feomi, whom he hugged so affectionately.

Perhaps she had also already been handed around, like a trophy.

No, she was seeing ghosts. Benu had introduced her to his friend and nothing else, it was actually a nice gesture.

★ ★ ★

What was reality? The mast of the traffic light at the intersection. The steel felt cool when Juno touched it with her hand, and when she knocked against it, she noticed that the mast was hollow. Reality was something that one could determine.

★ ★ ★

Reality on 5 February 2023 was three new tattoos.

Once again by a tattoo artist, the young art student from Frankfurt. Juno liked his style, he made nice drawings, funny animals and serious flowers, and also a lot of letters, words or sayings. One said 'youth'.

There was a star on her right upper thigh; over it, in baroque font: 'dolce vita'.

She had selected this from his flashes.

In a certain sense it was true, she had a sweet life.

What are you doing right now?

> I'm lying in bed and writing, it's going to
> be a theatre piece.
> It's crazy that I can just do something
> like that.
> Write a play about everything that's
> happening in my life and in general.

It's this very text here. We see it before us, it's no longer a
theatre piece, and if you wanted to make one out of it, you'd
really have to shorten everything.

Juno Isabella Flock always writes in bed between 7 and
8 a.m.; a little later, she goes off to dance, sometimes she also
writes in the evenings or at night.

It's a text about tattoos, the planet Melancholia, about
older women, love scammers, Nigeria.

It's a text about you, with whom I'm chatting.

> About my tattoos.
> *Smiley*

Nice! Lol!
Laughing smiley
You can write a whole book
About that?

> Well I'm expanding all of it a bit
> to other areas,
> I'll tell you more soon.

That was the truth, that Juno had still not told Benu the truth; he with whom she was chatting and telephoning via video call. That the text she was writing was about how she was chatting with him.

The truth was that she was still lying to him.

She was exploiting him; she had turned the circumstances around.

In fact, she would have to pay Benu a share if she earned anything from this text later on.

The scammer got his money. This time for fair work.

That was cynical.

★ ★ ★

And two more tattoos.

Juno travelled to the Südvorstadt, climbed up to the fourth floor, to an apartment in which there was a small tattoo studio. The tattoo artist was a young, polite person with short hair and many tattoos. They said hello.

She climbed onto the table again and it started again.

She got a wild bee on her right arm.

Earlier, Juno had sent the tattoo artist a photo of a wild bee that she had found on the internet. There were many different types of wild bees; some had thick fur, and some flew around almost naked. Juno chose a furry bee, which was diagonally in the air in the photo.

Also, the word 'Truth' on her left calf.

The tattoo artist had created the font specially for Juno; curving letters made from tiny dots.

Juno felt the needles; they were shooting audacity into her.

And love. And truth. And the friendly nature of the bee.

Only slight pain, just concentration and handiwork. The buzzing of the tattoo machine. Sometimes they talked while the tattoo artist was doing his work.

About music, what they liked, or about money. Whether they could live on what they were making.

Some of the time, yes.

Their needs weren't so great.

And why a wild bee? asked the tattoo artist.

We recently had one as our guest, said Juno.

And that it had been nice to make its life a bit more pleasant.

In contrast to honeybees, wild bees don't produce anything, they just live to lay their eggs in a hole and store food for the larvae.

That's all, said Juno on the table, then they die.

And that this touched her somehow. A crass form of frugality.

And yet we need them in nature, said the tattoo artist.

Of course. They pollinate plants. Honeybees, by contrast, are a kind of luxury variant; honey is something that flows out of them during their lives. An excess.

And of course we harvest that, said the tattoo artist.

An hour later, the wild bee flew and flew.

Juno looked at herself in the mirror. The arm where the bee lived now.

And then her legs. Her legs were more than one metre long. One of them was now decorated with a symbol. Truth. A symbol that it was true. That she, Juno, existed.

★ ★ ★

In the ballet studio, Ursi and the others intentionally didn't look at the tattoos when Juno stepped up to the barre; at least that's what Juno thought because they were quieter than usual.

But perhaps that wasn't right.

She was wearing a sleeveless jersey and capri-length leggings that showed her calves. When she came to class with the first tattoos, perhaps the others thought these would be the only ones. But now there were many.

Later, in a private lesson with Naïs – Juno wanted to practise her piqués on pointe; she did not push her free leg firmly enough from the floor and she did not shift her body weight to the passé, but instead always tipped in the other direction, away from her free leg – Juno pointed out the new tattoos.

I will cover them with make-up for the show, she said to Naïs. The ballet school was planning its annual summer celebration, the first one after three years' break due to the pandemic.

It was clear that everyone in the group would participate. It didn't matter to anyone that they were all over fifty.

Class had not begun yet. Juno crouched on the floor, tying the ribbons of her pointe shoes.

But Naïs asked, Why would you do that? And that the tattoos looked good. When you're over fifty, you can do anything, said Naïs, it doesn't matter what other people think.

Juno had never thought about things like this. She stretched her calves, did some lunges, saw how far down towards the floor she came. In the mirror, when she looked at her body, not a lot had changed.

People said that ballet keeps you young because you have to keep your whole body upright all the time, up to your face, which was always a bit tense because of the posture. Nothing in your face could sink because everything was tied down so tightly.

Then Naïs told her about the daughter of a dancer who had been cutting her arms for three years.

Then I'd rather see tattoos, said Naïs.

Juno asked herself whether the tattoos served a purpose for her, whether they were a substitute for something else.

She stood facing the barre, pressed her feet forward on the instep, balanced the weight of her body precisely over that, as one does.

It was like being a waving birch tree. The feeling quickly became addictive.

They smiled at each other and began the class.

The tattoos undulated over her muscles.

Juno tensed her body, began to fly.

At the summer celebration, they would dance the *Pas de Quatre* by Jules Perrot. A famous piece from 1845, created for the four most famous dancers in the Western world at that time. Marie Taglioni, Carlotta Grisi, Lucile Grahn and Fanny Cerrito.

They were superstars then. They met and appeared together for the first time at the premiere of the piece. That was a sensation.

Juno was supposed to dance the part of Marie Taglioni.

There was no plot in the piece, just a situation: four women danced together. Geometric patterns, rectangles, circles, diagonals.

Planets that met and almost collided.

Four friends who play with each other, chase each other in a way, romp on a planet.

Four souls. Four souls who are still alive.

Juno had read a lot about ballet when she was still in school. There was no internet, she had to go to the bookshop and examine the catalogues there. *Reclam, Tanzgeschichte. Die Geschichte des Balletts. Bühnentanz von den Anfängen bis zur Gegenwart.* For a while, she drove her parents crazy, because she had her head in these books, even at the dinner table, and she would read passages out loud.

She had also taken classes. In a nearby town there was a ballet school; she was told that you needed ballet if you wanted to be an actress. But she had already given up on those plans. Or maybe she hadn't. The ballet teacher was enthusiastic about Juno; such long legs, such beautiful, strong feet, so much musicality; she had been born a dancer!

It just looks that way, said Juno.

Later on, the teacher had also seen that something was not right. When Juno was supposed to hold her hands in front of her navel, she held them much higher, in front of her chest. She couldn't judge spaces and distances; during the exercises in the middle of the room, she always got the feeling that the other dancers were about to bump into her. Her paths across the room were strangely bent, she couldn't hold a diagonal. Maybe something was wrong with her eyes. She could only dance well when she was dancing by herself in the studio. At some point, she stopped taking lessons.

Too bad, said the teacher. But perhaps you can go into vaudeville, take acrobatics courses.

I'd rather not, said Juno.

* * *

Now Juno trained every day. Meanwhile, she was much better able to hold a diagonal and estimate the distances to other people. Maybe it was a question of age. And the fact that Juno really didn't care whether she kept to the diagonals or not.

Rehearsals were at least twice a week, also on Saturdays and Sundays; they often lasted until late in the evening.

Sometimes, Juno looked at her fellow dancers when they were standing around in the studio during a break, out of breath, listening to the improvements that Naïs was suggesting, and she sought something in their faces, but she didn't know what she was seeking.

A few wrinkles or those little indentations below the corners of the mouth because the skin gets less elastic and starts to hang, and that's why it formed the indentations, but that's not what she was searching for.

On Instagram, Juno had seen reels where young women demonstrated how you could get rid of the indentations with face exercises.

But the women here, in her dance group, didn't have these indentations anyway.

Their skin was stretched so tightly over their cheekbones that nothing could hang down.

It was possible that Juno was looking for a point in the face that would betray how permeable they were for everything still to come.

And for everything that lay behind them.

A membrane through which something was glowing.

She sent Benu a photo of her pointe shoes, without her feet in them.

> They look very nice,
> but very small.
>
> And yet my feet are pretty large.
>
> *The Scream-by-Edvard-Munch-emoji*

Does it hurt when you dance in them?

> Not when you have the right shoes and
> good technique.
> It's like a drug. After the first few steps
> I get high.

At first, Juno felt a bit uncomfortable talking about ballet with Benu. Ballet was widespread around the world, ballet was more colonial than the strongest colonial power ever was, ballet was everywhere, like birds and mosquitoes.

The super-white ballet. Juno knew almost everything about it.

Ballet was brimming with racist stereotypes (*Nutcracker, Le Corsaire, La Bayadère, Don Quixote*).

Until the 2000s, all of these pieces that featured Black-face (*Le Corsaire, La Bayadère, Nutcracker*) were played in the big traditional opera houses; and up until 2019 at the Bolshoi (*Nutcracker*).

There were many strong female figures in these pieces, and often the ballets were radical critiques of class society; often they were directed against the nobility (*Giselle, Romeo and Juliet*).

The European dance world of the eighteenth and nineteenth centuries was anything but bourgeois. In some ways it was a bit like the circus, full of migratory, anarchistic people who never wanted to live like the bourgeoisie.

But that didn't make the racism in the ballets any better.

And there were other things you could criticize about ballet, the stereotypical female ideal of beauty, the stereotypical picture of men. Knights, princes, the power to jump, muscles.

But when you're dancing, you leave the Earth's atmosphere;

that's how it was. Juno couldn't stop thinking about that; sometimes she had the feeling that she was only real in the ballet studio.

As if she wanted to excuse the white ballet, she wrote to Benu a lot about it.

> I actually only like the dancing itself, the technique.
>
> The pieces don't interest me much, but for Giselle, Swan Lake, Romeo and Juliet.
> Because everything ends so mercilessly there.

Benu had heard of *Swan Lake* and of *Romeo and Juliet*, but he wasn't familiar with *Giselle*.

> It's about a young woman who is being led on by a man, a kind of dark fairy tale. The man is a powerful prince and promises to marry her, but he's already long since engaged to a countess.
> For him, it was just a game. When Giselle realizes this, she dances through the whole party and dies.
> Of a broken heart, it is said. Later, the prince has a guilty conscience, he wants to visit Giselle's grave and he gets lost in the forest. He meets the Wilis, the spirits of women who died from lovesickness.

The prince has to dance with them until
he falls over dead, but Giselle is among
the Wilis. She forgives him and casts a
spell that protects him. He is allowed to
leave as dawn breaks.

Wow, a sad story.
Sad smiley with tears

Yeah, someone always has to die in
stories like that.
Otherwise, it doesn't draw people in.

The prince really takes something on when he's
wandering through the forest at night.

Only unfortunately it's too late for his
courage.

Benu sent one of those heart emojis.
The heart that's broken in the middle.

EIGHT

Rehearse, dance, rehearse.

Juno had to plan her next performances, the guest performances in Munich were coming up. The theatre had obtained a guest subsidy for her, she was earning money for the performance; it could be more, but it was okay. She even had a travel expense budget. There were three of them, the instruments had to go along, and the costumes. They needed a car and someone to drive it, as none of them had a driver's licence.

When would she buy supplies for Jupiter?

She had to write e-mails, scrutinize the numbers for the budget, and the next production was already lined up, an audio walk through the Leipzig alluvial forest, again with Tristan and Phoebus, in September. Juno had written a work about a modern Artemis who lived in a dystopian forest; Phoebus had made it into a lovely radio play. Juno obtained financial support from the city's Ministry of Culture, but nothing came from the Cultural Foundation of the Free State of Saxony; the project had to make do with half the planned funds.

Juno recalculated everything, re-did the budget, pushed sums back and forth. Sennheiser was donating twelve sets of headphones, which saved them something. They needed project management for their next pieces, as the business side was becoming overwhelming.

Juno's head was pounding; in the evening, she just threw herself in front of her laptop and opened Instagram.

There was Madonna with bleached eyebrows and a pointy chin at the Grammy Awards – so what? Was that all?

It caused an uproar on social media.

In the photos, Madonna's face was heart-shaped and smooth, her cheeks round and pulled upwards, and she didn't have a single wrinkle. There was even a report about it on TV, on *Hallo Deutschland*, which Juno sometimes watched on the internet late at night while she was stretching. When you were stretching, you needed something that didn't require too much concentration but that you could still follow.

Everyone said Madonna was deceiving people with this heart-shaped face.

It wasn't real, this face.

That's especially what women around forty said on Facebook.

Juno kept calculating the numbers for the budget; it wasn't really money that was motivating her. What motivated her, anyway? Energy.

An excess of energy generates a bang, a shock or a fire.

This was February 2023, a month with numbers.

A month in which the war in Ukraine had already been raging for a year.

A month in which there were elections in Nigeria. Juno had no concept of Nigeria's election system, of Nigeria's political system in general.

She visited Jupiter in his room, as always, brought him a pizza. The next day, chicken sausage in puff pastry; Wednesdays, spinach bites from the snack shelf in the supermarket, then their account was empty again.

Juno didn't care what Madonna looked like.

Masses of first-time voters had registered for the elections in Nigeria; Juno read that in *Die Zeit online*. Ninety million people were entitled to vote, of these, almost half were under thirty-five.

Die Zeit wrote that hopefully young people in Nigeria wanted to change something in their country. The inflation rate was 22 per cent, about half the population lived below the national poverty line. Although Nigeria has the largest economy on the African continent.

That was February 2023.

★ ★ ★

And how small the circles in which she was moving were by comparison. The path she was treading was the one from the dance studio to home, not even a mile. And yet half a world. The complex with the new buildings, the Karlbrücke over the White Elster River, you could see the stars very well here. But not tonight, it was cloudy.

A fox crossed the street, then two raccoons; that was all.

The neighbourhood was large enough to accommodate all of this without attracting attention. The constellations. Being awake. The injustice in the world. Jupiter, the mighty storm that was breaking over him, the red eye that you saw in every picture.

She had turned into the Könneritzstraße, passed by the round wooden bench that was built around a small plane tree in front of the supermarket. A young woman and a young man crouched on the seat, under the small leafy roof, both of them half sitting, half lying down; the woman had pulled her knees up to her chest. Next to them was one of those big shopping bags made of recycled plastic.

As Juno approached, she could see that the woman was shivering. The man lit a cigarette. Their age was difficult to estimate. They looked battered but they were wearing stylish, clean clothing.

Juno passed by them. The young woman looked at her, but didn't say anything.

Juno had hardly moved when she heard the two talking softly. When she turned around, she saw that they were following her.

Their quick steps.

Juno kept up her pace. She didn't want to run away, especially not from such young people.

Soon, the three of them were walking next to each other.

First, Juno looked at them from the side, annoyed.

Neither of them seemed to notice.

The young woman was carrying the bag over her shoulder. It was rubbing against her jacket, scratch, scratch.

Do you have some money for us? she asked finally, in English with a Spanish accent.

Juno took a closer look at both of them. They were good-looking, no missing teeth, they didn't seem like the usual homeless.

I'm sorry, said Juno.

Not for you, she thought. She didn't have much money in her wallet anyway.

They passed the bank where she had her account. The little vestibule with the ATMs was lit up in neon yellow.

How would it feel, thought Juno, to take twenty euros out of the ATM and hand it over to them? Or maybe fifty euros.

For a brief moment, she wanted to do something

flamboyant, excessive, so that they would certainly be ashamed. The two of them remained at her side, not intrusively. More like two small moons orbiting the sun with Juno.

What are your names? she asked at some point.

Pirwa, said the woman; Cielo, the young man.

Nice names, said Juno, and Pirwa said that her name came from the Inca culture. She was from Spain, but her mother had named all of her children after Inca gods. Juno said she thought that was a wonderful idea, but Pirwa didn't seem to care, her face remained expressionless.

And what's going to happen now, Pirwa? Juno didn't say that out loud.

You're taking drugs and travelling through Europe. That's not a good plan in the long run. If you have bad luck, you'll be a toothless wreck in two or three years. Or perhaps even dead, Pirwa. Then all your beauty would be for nothing. Or maybe this was a small, adventurous phase in your life and in two years you'll be back in your safe, stylish life somewhere in the world and then look back on this crazy time with a shudder.

And maybe that would be even worse.

Juno let this idea circle in her head and played with it a little, with pleasure, as if it were something physical; a ball that rolled gently back and forth in her head. The colourful neon advertisement in a bar shone back at them. Juno passed by here often; in summer people sat at little wooden tables on the pavement, but now it was too cold for that. She had never gone into the bar.

Let's go, we're going in, she said. It was just as excessive an idea as the one about the bank and the fifty euros, but more realistic. She didn't wait to see what Pirwa and Cielo would say; she simply opened the door. Inside it was smoky, the bar wasn't very big. Drunken men and women were sitting on chairs and benches everywhere, with countless glasses and bottles in front of them on the small tables. There was loud music, an expressionless younger man with longish hair stood behind the bar. Two barstools were free. Pirwa and Cielo climbed up on them, Juno leaned on the bar and ordered three beers. She didn't even have to turn around to know that they were being watched. People had turned to look at them as soon as they came in. A not-so-young woman with two young people. Everyone probably thought she was the mother. She was alarmingly unconcerned. Think what you will. Juno drank half of her bottle quickly and felt the strange lightness of alcohol, actually an oily heaviness, go to her head.

They talked a little about Pirwa's mother. Juno was interested in her because she had given her children names from Inca mythology. Pirwa told her that her mother had owned a big beauty parlour in Barcelona and raised her children by herself after their father simply disappeared. But now she was old and sick, and she had sold the beauty parlour.

It made her rich, said Pirwa, and she had bought a house with a pool.

How old is she? asked Juno. Pirwa responded: Sixty-two.

Juno was shocked. She'd thought 'old' meant at least seventy.

Pirwa had turned towards her. Juno couldn't tell if she had taken drugs, she didn't have enough experience for that. Her gaze looked clear. She and Cielo didn't seem to think it was unusual to be sitting in a bar with a woman who was almost the same age as Pirwa's mother.

Suddenly, the bartender put three shot glasses filled to the rim on the bar in front of them.

Sliwowitz, he said, it's on the house, it's our ten-year anniversary this week.

Pirwa and Cielo looked pleased and toasted the bartender.

Juno hesitated for a moment. Schnapps, that would really do her in. What she had told Benu about alcohol was actually true.

Oh well. She even said that out loud. The bartender grinned. She emptied the glass at one go as the others had done and felt the burning warmth running into her stomach.

Do you live alone? asked Cielo suddenly.

At first, Juno thought she'd misunderstood, it was a question that she automatically associated with the love scammers.

No, she said then. I live with Jupiter, the great Jupiter.

Pirwa and Cielo looked amused. Juno noticed that she was already drunk, she hadn't eaten anything since midday.

Good that Benu didn't see her; she was smiling to herself.

Did you know that Jupiter protects the Earth against asteroid collisions with his gravitational power? she said then.

If Jupiter didn't exist, we probably wouldn't be here.

Because there would have been constant hail from the sky and humankind probably wouldn't even have developed.

Pirwa and Cielo's eyes got big, but they didn't say much about this.

The bartender put three more Sliwowitz on the bar. Juno raised her glass.

Here's to Jupiter, she said.

Cheers, Jupiter! cried Pirwa and Cielo, and all three of them laughed and downed the schnapps. Pirwa and Cielo looked amused again. Maybe they thought she was a whimsical older woman.

What if that's right? thought Juno.

Suddenly Cielo took her hands in his; it happened so fast that Juno couldn't pull her hands away. Cielo's skin felt raw. He was smiling, but it was a devilish grin.

Could we stay with you tonight?

It sounded more like a suggestion than a question.

Cielo was holding her hands firmly, almost on the wrists. Juno was probably too drunk to find this strange.

Or she was too surprised.

That's not a good idea, she said. You see, Jupiter is very sick. Big old Jupiter. That he of all people is sick! Hopefully his gravitational field won't break down. Otherwise, the asteroids will come.

Furthermore – Juno tried not to seem drunk – she tried to speak clearly – we don't have any space.

Cielo had let go of her hands and Juno was rummaging in her wallet for that last bit of money for the beers and the tip. She laid it on the bar.

And another thing, there is only one person I love, she said to Cielo, and only he may hold my hands.

She had to try hard not to slur her words.

It was only a joke, said Cielo.

I know, said Juno.

Outside on the street, she showed them the stop for the bus to Connewitz; they would find other young people there who would offer them a place to sleep.

Just talk to someone your age, said Juno, I'm sure it will all work out.

She still had to try hard not to seem drunk. Don't sway, don't grin too wide. It was stressful. She waved to both of them when they were standing across the street at the bus stop, and Pirwa and Cielo waved back.

On the way home, she noticed how dizzy she was. My poor body! Suddenly, she wished that she had taken Pirwa and Cielo home. Not into the apartment, just up to the front door. They could have supported her, drunk as she was.

Just having people around her for a change, people to take care of her. Even for a few minutes. That would actually be really nice, she thought.

Jupiter was already in bed, but he wasn't sleeping yet; he turned to her drowsily.

Juno sat on the edge of the bed, stroked his head.

She was feeling a bit more sober, and she was happy about that. Well? she said, and Jupiter also said, Well? He asked her how dance class was.

It was good, responded Juno. She didn't trust herself to tell him the truth, and she felt bad for that. She said that she'd briefly gone to a bar with some people from the group.

I drank schnapps.

At least part of the truth.

Jupiter laughed. You and schnapps.

There was live music in the bar, said Juno; she also danced, forgot the time.

That's nice, said Jupiter. A smile flitted across his face, perhaps he looked a little wistful.

Do you remember how we were together in that club once upon a time? she asked, and Jupiter laughed again.

Juno had just moved to Leipzig; they hadn't known each other long. Jupiter's illness had not yet been diagnosed.

Juno missed dancing from before; for a while she had danced through the night in discotheques, and really danced, without interruption. Jupiter couldn't dance well and didn't like to dance, but he came to the club with her without complaining, just to please her.

They were almost entirely alone; the club was empty, and the two of them spent the whole night on the dance floor.

She had watched Jupiter's stamping movements with great emotion, he was already limping then.

Again and again, he lost the rhythm, caught himself again, Juno saw how hard he was trying. At first, he was tense, inhibited, but at some point, something in him let go. He closed his eyes, let his arms fly, swayed back and forth in the red and blue lights.

Jupiter had danced and danced; the eye of the storm swirled around.

Juno, the probe that was flying around him, had filmed everything.

They held each other for a long time. They held each other tightly; it wasn't clear who was holding whom.

Then Juno went into her room, switched on the little lamp.

★ ★ ★

Madonna's face was still everywhere. A male plastic surgeon from the USA put a YouTube video online: Madonna's face. Green markings where the expert suspected she had had work done: neck, cheeks, forehead, eyelids, lips.

During a facelift, the skin on the face that hung down was pulled diagonally upwards, the excess cut off, the skin sewed to the temples and under the ear. The expert suspected that Madonna had had her first facelift at thirty. More marked photos followed: Madonna before and after.

In the caption, there was a list of all the procedures including hyaluronic acid fillers; the prices were also listed.

Then the total popped up; about three-quarters of a million dollars.

Juno made the financial plan for the next performance.

She conjured some pizzas for Jupi from her shopping bag.

One of her Facebook friends posted a photo of Madonna at the Grammys, Madonna with her youthful, heart-shaped face.

The friend wrote that he thought Madonna looked good that way, and Juno liked the post. A few women commented that, as an older woman, one should age with dignity. Their profile pictures indicated that they were younger.

Juno wrote a long, biting commentary about the term 'dignity', but did not post it.

Once again, she showed Benu her new tattoos; another video call, she held her arm with the wild bee up to the camera.

Wow, said Benu, it's beautiful. Now you have a lot more tattoos than I do.

Usually they talked this way; a kind of small talk that gave the illusion of depth because it didn't say much about anything. What could Juno say? As a white, European woman, there wasn't much to say after she had seen the documentaries about the women on holiday in Kenya and Ghana. And because, at the same time, she was rather familiar with love scamming. And what could she say without giving herself away? Without accidentally telling him something about her real life? There wasn't much there either.

Everything on Earth consisted of exploitation systems; there wasn't anything that was done just so, without compensation, without a purpose that in the end brought in money.

Money was the fourth natural force, after fire, the big bang and vibration, arising from a surplus of energy.

Or rather the longing for money, the need.

Sometimes Juno thought about having the word 'money' tattooed on one of her legs.

★ ★ ★

How far had she already gone and how would she get out of the story, back into normality?

Ha ha, what normality, Juno?

Benu had still never attempted to ask her for money. Would that happen later? What would happen later in this story?

Next, there were two curious sentences.

It was after eleven, the electricity in Benu's room had gone out again, the candle flickered. Benu told her he had to go to Port Harcourt because of a job, something at the airport, a security position. He would have to move for the job.

And would you like to do that? Would you like to move away?

Benu was smoking, as always. Smoke curled around him, dimming the candlelight.

No, he said, everything is much worse there than here. He meant his city.

It's bleak and dangerous in Port Harcourt; there are always shootings.

Then he said that Nigeria was simply a horrible country.

He didn't look at her; his gaze wandered through the room, stopped somewhere.

This country doesn't do anything for its people, said Benu, and once again, Juno didn't know what to say.

That you should engage yourself politically.

That you should start a revolution.

That someone had to do something.

She didn't say any of that because maybe it was also senseless bullshit that came out of her mouth, a mouth in Germany.

Juno said she was sorry.

Thank you, said Benu, that means a lot to me.

Then he said something else.

You look so nice.

You can't ever be evil.

He said.

NINE

Juno travelled back to the mountains.

Back to her mother's apartment, to her childhood room where the sofa was, the one that was once in the living room. It could be folded out; you could sleep quite well on it.

In Leipzig, the snow had long since thawed, but there was still snow on the ground here. A lot of grey sky hung over the mountains; you could only see the lower cliffs, the forests glinted darkly.

If the evening sky had been clear, you could have seen the constellation Leo directly overhead, with its brightest star, Regulus.

Over Central Europe, the lion is a horizontal rectangle. From its right side, a kind of neck leads upwards; a small head hangs above it. If you want to, you can make out a lion crouching on the ground.

Juno saw a swan or a reclining brachiosaurus. Once, when she checked timeanddate.com, she discovered that on this date, the lion was standing on its head over Nigeria. In Nigeria, it would be even harder to see a lion in the figure.

Nevertheless, the constellation was called Leo around the world.

Each day, Juno took a walk with her friend's dog; she knew the woman from before. Her friend had to go into the office during the day and she was happy that Juno could take the dog out. A sheepdog mongrel.

His name was Ninto.

Juno liked to call out his name; she could hold the second *n* in the front on her tongue for a moment, a feeling like sitting on a swing. And for another thing, the sound ended with this dark *o* like her own name.

And Ninto seemed to like it when she called him; he came right away, always jumping towards her, but Juno did not call him very often. She would rather let Ninto dash across the wide, snow-covered fields, in the middle of town, between the mountain cliffs.

Sometimes she wrote to Benu, sent a few photos.

Wow, so much snow!

I'm sinking down into it.

Is that your dog?

No, it's my friend's dog.
He flips out in the snow, rolls around in it, I could watch him for ever.
I want a dog like that.
I want to be a dog like that.

Juno had been thinking about getting a dog from the animal shelter for a while. In the past, she hadn't liked dogs, especially not large ones. She had always thought they were nervous nuisances. But dogs were gentle and cautious like thick, big clouds. Recently, Juno had developed an eye for them.

A dog, never!
Laughing smiley
No one likes them here,
sometimes they bite.

> Dogs are revered in Germany, especially
> the little ones.
> People carry them in bags, take them to
> the office.
> Here in the mountains there are dogs
> that can rescue you in the snow;
> everybody could use a dog like that, a
> rescue dog.

What are they supposed to rescue you from?

> From everything.

The main thing: not from me.
GIF: big dog, gently nudging a canary
perched on the ground with its snout

> GIF: *white bull terrier, curling his lips away*
> *from his teeth so far that it looks like he's*
> *grinning broadly*

On one of these evenings, under the lights of the hut up there
on the peak of Mount Neuner, with the noises from the TV in
the living room next door audible, another request fluttered in.

A strange profile on Instagram.

Juno hadn't responded to any requests for a while
although sometimes it rained like the Perseids in her direct
messages.

The conversations with Benu were blowing enough

unrest into the stars, but here, at the foot of Mount Neuner, everything was halfway peaceful right now.

The season was not yet clearly recognizable.

Half winter, half spring; it had not yet been decided whether the brightness would break in at any moment or whether the days would remain in the long darkness for a while yet.

Juno took a quick look at the photo; it wasn't real, she had already forgotten what the man in it looked like.

Someone with sunglasses on his forehead.

She didn't ever read the name on the profile; the names were always the same.

Tanned, greying Titans.

What did the scammers think, what kind of taste did they think she had?

Juno would never have found a man like that attractive.

Are you married?

> No, I'm in the mountains right now with
> my two lovers, we're doing a kind of
> meditation camp.
>
> What do you mean by send a photo of us?
>
> Oh.

He meant a photo of how the three of them were having sex.

> In our camp we want to learn how we
> can have sex with just our souls.
> We have a master here, he's teaching us.
> We take a lot of drugs, sleep in an igloo,
> that's a house made of snow.

This time, the conversation ended because it wasn't a love scammer.

He believed everything Juno said and wanted to see it online.

He would even pay for that; did Juno have PayPal?

He sent her a dick pic.

A white dick, of course.

Juno had to laugh.

★ ★ ★

The next morning, she took a walk with Ninto; they took a little detour through town. In Leipzig, Juno always said she came from a village, but that wasn't entirely true. There was an ice-skating rink, an indoor swimming pool, hotels, a factory that made fine mechanical precision instruments, and a few farms.

She passed the train station; every hour, a train departed for the bigger town nearby, and another went to Tyrol. The little train station building was closed. That's where, for a while, Juno waited every day for the train to the other town, to the ballet school. Sometimes she smoked like everyone else in this austere grey room.

She and Ninto passed the kindergarten where she had played the crooked pine tree way back when. There was still a big garden, where once there had been a little playground carousel and a rectangular wading pool, plus a few swings. These had long since been replaced by wooden climbing structures and a basketball court. No children in sight.

At the celebration for her kindergarten class, before she went off to real school, there was another play. Some kind of flower fairy tale, but Juno didn't get a part.

You're strange, said one of the girls in the class to Juno. Juno remembered that well.

By the time she was in primary school, Juno herself thought she was strange. The other girls were always standing close together and whispering and giggling. In the winter, when the boys made as if they were going to throw snowballs at them, they screeched in pretend fright. Juno didn't understand why they did that.

Don't look at us so strangely, said a girl to her.

Juno could not tell from her face whether the girl meant that in a mean way or as a joke.

Jason, who had played St Nicholas at the Christmas party, told her that she looked scary.

Juno looked at herself in the mirror in the school toilets.

Two slight bulges at the top of her forehead. Perhaps she would soon grow horns.

You squint, said Jason.

You run awkwardly, said one of the girls.

Another boy said she was a witch.

Juno still doesn't fit in well with the class, it said in her first report card in high school under 'remarks'.

Don't be so complicated, then everything is easier, said her mother. Your friends are so nice.

Juno tried.

When she played at being an uncomplicated person, most people believed her.

But they are not my friends, she said to her mother.

They turned around and walked back down the main street; it was too loud for Ninto. They turned into a path that led into a little forest. Juno had been here often. A strange, deserted place, a little bit enchanted, the trees grew wild, all kinds mixed together, and between them, rampant under-growth. Sometimes unfamiliar, enticing berries hung over the path. They stopped in front of a big pine and Juno let Ninto off the lead. Right away, he started snuffling around the trunk of a pine. He wagged his tail happily and explored the surrounding trees.

Nothing had changed. Juno walked once around the pine and looked up, the two boards were still there. They had already been there when she built the treehouse with Nyx. 'Treehouse' might be overstating things a bit; they climbed up and placed four additional boards across the two that were already screwed to the trunk and branches; they tied the new boards tight with a climbing rope. It was a bit shaky, but it held well. She had met Nyx in the confirmation class; usually they skipped, and after three months, they both left the group. Their parents had grumbled but given in, in the end. Nyx lived at the other end of town and wore his hair long. At that time, that was enough to ensure that he was periodically beaten up by the other boys from town.

They slept with each other up here; it was the first time for both of them, it was a bit complicated on the shaky boards.

At some point, Aamon and Salvan had destroyed the tree-house. They were drunk; they climbed up the trunk and cut the rope with a knife, just like that, without telling anyone. The boards landed on the ground next to Juno and Nyx. Nyx was just as drunk, Juno only a little.

She cried: Are you crazy? Juno remembered all of this happening as if in slow motion: the splintered branches flew towards them very slowly like asteroids that were about to hit the Earth.

Somehow, everything escalated; later on nobody could

say precisely why. They went into the little forest in a big group, more or less drunk, and someone, probably Aamon, started a fight. By then, most of the others were gone.

Juno knew Aamon and Salvan from the confirmation class, a doctor's son and the son of the owner of the largest hotel in town.

Sometimes they also crossed paths in the school bus.

Oh no, here comes the crazy girl! Sometimes Aamon yelled that across the whole bus.

And that ugly haircut! Please don't make me look at it!

* * *

Sometimes things just escalate, and they can't be resolved retrospectively, with more clarity about what exactly happened and why.

You said, then I said, and therefore you did that. And so on.

But perhaps that was too easy.

Maybe there were just good and bad people.

The next morning, Juno had several big bruises on her body, and they had cut Nyx's hair off.

Where did they get scissors that fast? Juno only thought about that later. Or did they just carry scissors with them, in their trouser pocket or jacket pocket? There were people like that.

No question mark. A full stop.

Aamon and Salvan were both dead.

Juno had seen Salvan's obituary in the newspaper when she was visiting her mother. Leukaemia at thirty-two.

That was a while ago already; at the time, she was living in Berlin.

Probably a consequence of Chernobyl, said her mother. Aamon had died a little earlier, contaminated ecstasy.

There was an article in the regional newspaper; her mother sent it to her in the post. There was even a paragraph about Aamon in an article in *Der Spiegel* about the dangers of synthetic drugs.

Frequently, Juno had noted that she felt a kind of strange satisfaction when she thought about these two deaths. And again now.

And yet they spooked her.

She thought about Justine from *Melancholia*. How in the early phase of her depression, she wasn't weak and dejected, but mean-spirited and hard-boiled. Ice-cold, actually. Juno could understand that.

She called for Ninto, it was already late; she had to take him back to her friend soon. She smiled at him as he leapt blithely and looked at her expectantly.

The spook with the ice-cold thoughts was gone again.

You're a good boy, she said, scratching Ninto behind the ears. He didn't know anything about people. How they could be. Briefly, a thought crossed her mind.

That it would have been nice if she'd had a Ninto at that time.

★ ★ ★

Dogs would play a role in her life, that much was already clear. Later, much later in Leipzig when all of this was over, Benu a satellite that had got lost –

Later, she, Juno Isabella Flock, would play with a dog in her apartment. Relaxed and happy.

The dog's name was Sora; that was Japanese for 'sky'.

Sora would spend two weeks with Juno and Jupiter.

In the evening, she and Sora would play in Jupiter's room. Juno would throw a ball, and Sora would chase it down. Sora would hold the ball in his mouth and each time he wanted Juno to pull it away from him and throw it again.

Jupiter watches from his bed and thinks it's sweet.

They stand in the middle of the room and fight for the ball; Sora pulls, Juno doesn't let go, Sora wags his tail and is happy.

Once, when Juno nearly has the ball, Sora tries to adjust his bite a little and jumps with his teeth very close to Juno's finger. Sora misjudges a bit, one of his sharp teeth catches in Juno's middle finger, right below the nailbed.

It's only a small scratch, but it bleeds copiously. Juno cries ouch and Sora is sorry right away. He stops playing, crawls towards Juno with his hind legs stretched out, and looks up at her from below.

It's okay, says Juno, I know that you didn't mean to do it. She strokes Sora so that he calms down.

The dog belongs to her friend Naïs, her ballet teacher, and Naïs's boyfriend; a Jack Russell terrier.

Naïs and her boyfriend will have flown off to Japan this summer.

Juno loves the dog with a vehemence that scrambles a few things in the world each time.

Sora keeps watch over her, follows her everywhere, brings her his toys, takes one of her socks into his basket every night.

Juno will write to Naïs on WhatsApp, just to ask, for caution's sake, whether the dog has had his rabies injections.

When it comes to rabies, Juno is incredibly cautious; it's irrational, she knows, because rabies no longer exists in Central Europe. Germany has been free of rabies since 2008.

But nevertheless.

In her town in the mountains, a dog died from rabies once upon a time. When it happened, people said that he turned in circles for four days and couldn't do anything about it. Soon blood was running from his ears; everyone talked about it then.

Juno didn't see the dog.

The older people in the town said that if a person got rabies, first he would walk backwards and then litres of spit would collect in his mouth, which would ultimately suffocate him.

Naïs's boyfriend writes: Sorry, we didn't get him the second injection yet!

Shortly after that, Naïs writes yes, we did get him the second injection.

Juno will have slept poorly on this evening in summer, when Benu is just another satellite out of service and she, Juno, now in an orbit of her own, is not sending out any more data.

The next morning, she will go to the urgent care clinic on the corner; she will spend two hours in the waiting room. You can hear the clock on the wall ticking. Can it be, thinks Juno, that she is developing irrational fears? Yes, it can be.

Sora is at home with Jupiter.

The doctor will tell her what she already knew.

No reason to worry as long as you know the dog's history.

He says that rabies is only a problem in Africa, sometimes in Asia; each year, 21,000 people die from rabies, the majority of them children.

He was in the Congo a few times, with Médecins Sans Frontières. Children are bitten most often by rabid dogs; it always affects the most vulnerable, says the doctor.

But there's nothing more to do here.

Juno will think that she's a Western hypochondriac, endlessly exaggerating her fear.

Juno will think that she can no longer distinguish reality from what's going on inside her head.

And that Benu too is just a phantom.

In the process, Juno had learned this much earlier: to think that some things that she actually experienced were only imaginary and didn't really take place at all.

That was a useful strategy, just like playing a normal, happy person in school.

Benu will be gone. Is there also a strategy for this? Juno had saved some chats as screenshots. Actually, this isn't a good move, as chats are like conversations; they should go with the wind and only the memory of them should remain. Nevertheless, she will have the chats. Proof that Benu really existed. That he was present; far away, but still.

This occurs once again to Juno, almost at the end of the story.

Pictures of Men in Love

A performer, preferably a woman,
makes the movements and gestures

Man in love, who has a buzz saw on his belt.

Man in love, who is sitting at a table and trying to draw a butterfly on a piece of paper.

Man in love, kicking the air with his foot.

Man in love, who is painting his toenails.

Man in love, who was just hit by a shot.

Man in love, who is spooning out a cup of rice.

Man in love, who keeps hanging up on someone on his phone.

Man in love, who sits on the floor in the middle of the room and cries.

TEN

She still knew precisely how it was.

The spring sunshine shone especially brightly, like it always does at the end of March, the beginning of April. Furthermore, Delta Cephei exploded again; that happened every five days, then it shrank again, and so on, from the beginning.

So, it was not a moment that would have fallen outside the laws of physics, but nevertheless, Juno noticed it.

She shut the door of her room, eleven o'clock at night, pink light from the floor lamp fell on her face, she held her phone a little away from her.

The camera was already on; you could see her in demi-profile, not straight from the front but rather from the side.

Juno caught herself checking whether she looked okay. But what did that mean, looking okay? Looking so that no one would notice you? Or to the contrary, so that everyone would notice you? Too ugly, too beautiful, too conspicuous, too inconspicuous?

Looking like nothing. Looking like everything.

The phone rang, like always. The rippling pearly tone of the video call, like always.

Hi. Grin. Waving. How are you?

The candle was already flickering.

The light of the stars still didn't shine in their houses.

For a while, they talked softly, softly, so that Jupiter wouldn't hear anything. They talked about the coming spring; Juno talked about how she had been dancing.

Benu talked about how he had cooked stew, rice with meat and spinach, onions and tomatoes; his favourite dish, he said, but sometimes it was a bit bleak, always eating only stew.

Juno told him what she had eaten during the day: a salad and a roll, she had no time to cook.

You don't cook anyway, said Benu, and he laughed again.

He'd known for a long time that Juno didn't like to cook.

And then – but perhaps it was just an impression in her head but not actually something that really happened – Benu looked at her for longer than usual.

He held his head very straight, and he held her gaze; a smile flickered briefly across his face, then he looked serious again.

He looked and looked; it lasted a long time, approximately the same length of time that a fading shooting star was visible in the sky.

For the rest of the conversation he was quiet; he looked down at the floor sometimes, he seemed a little nervous.

It was all in her head.

They ended the call soon; once again, Juno didn't even know why they were having these video calls.

Usually, they only talked about food and what they'd done, what had happened that day.

Often, Juno didn't know what had happened.

Usually all the same things.

Then, in addition to the books about Africa, she was reading a lot about astronomy, everything all mixed up, non-fiction books for laypeople and specialized astrophysics books (Bergmann-Schäfer: *Experimental Physics Textbook*, Volume 8, *The Stars and Space*). They were from before, when she was *strange*. Her strange special interests. But they still made you a little cleverer.

She had learned that all insights about the universe came from stubborn evaluation of space, day by day, year by year.

Capturing light, evaluating it, then capturing it again, evaluating it again. This way, you discover deviations that might reveal themselves as facts.

From this tiny deviation in their video call – Benu looked different than he usually did – movements of an object that differed slightly from what had previously been recorded – no conclusions could be drawn yet, but it could be that Juno suspected something.

It wasn't even a theory, not even a suspicion, perhaps only a feeling; and a feeling was the most unreliable basis for examining reality.

The next morning, a message.

> Please don't be angry with me.
> I have to tell you something.

Pause, pause, pause.

> I think I've fallen in love with you.

Bam.

Some kind of bright explosion, perhaps space was contracting again.

Lie deceit Kenya white lady ocean come on sex loverboy
money hunger old lady shame what no no no
The end. Block.

Hey, are you still there?

Juno waited ten minutes.

I don't like that you say things like that
to me.
That we're starting to talk to each other
that way.

Are you angry?
Why?

This sounds strange to me.
You want me to become some kind of
Sugar Mama for you. That's what it
sounds like to me.
You think you can sell yourself to me.
That makes me angry!

And you think that I need this!
I don't, so that that's clear.

The weight of geological plates as they press against each other.
The African plate, the European plate.
There was no earthquake, just a big emptiness in the room.

No, I don't want to sell myself to you.
It was a compliment, nothing else.
Sorry, I didn't want to annoy you.

Pause.
Pause.
Pause.

      I just like how you are.
      How you look.
      You're so funny and a little special.

      And I like how you talk.

            Wow, but you HAVE annoyed me!

      You always told me about
      your lovers.
      I thought there's nothing bad about this!

            Even if I wanted to, you're much too
            young for me, and also very far away!
            And now goodbye for today.

Juno didn't believe any of that at all, Benu.

Who even writes something like that these days? I think I've fallen in love with you.

Only love scammers do that.

Now you wanted to get your money, Benu.

Juno, your Sugar Mama, should pay you something every month. No idea what the object of the trade should be, secret meetings on the screen?

            Also, I'm in a severe depressive phase
            right now, nothing interests me less than
            being in love.

And all that wasn't a lie, Benu. All of that was true. Juno had once secretly written a poem: 'I have a place between the ribs. My heart flutters there, you see it / or you don't see it.'

It would have been easier and better to keep lying, perhaps like this:

What do you mean by 'in love'?
In our culture we aren't familiar with
these words, there's only 'hate'.

That's nice of you, but thank you, I'm
in a relationship with the chief of an
international petrochemical company,
he pays for my apartment.

Oh, how nice, but my boyfriend is
the boss of the largest drug cartel in
Chemnitz. It's better if we don't say the
'in love' part if you value your life.
He always checks my chats and he has
connections around the world.

Instead of that:

And also, how do you imagine this
working?
That I fly to Nigeria with a lot of money
in my pocket? Or that you come to
Germany and I support you?

Don't even try.
Otherwise, I'll delete your number.
Do you understand?

★ ★ ★

You think I'm really rich, like everyone in Germany.

A business lady.

You don't understand anything.

You have no idea about Europe.

You have no idea about me.

You don't even know my name.

Juno wrote this and then deleted it.

She had silenced her phone so that she didn't hear when he wrote to her.

Benu's notifications popped up on the lock screen, one after another, Juno could touch and read them without marking them as read. What was this function for, anyway?

So that you could take your time and think up good answers?

Wasn't an answer thought out in advance also a form of lying?

She took her phone, opened Benu's profile and went to the contact information.

Profile picture, telephone number, the area code for Nigeria, she scrolled down to 'Block contact'. Briefly, she held her index finger over the field. Then she pulled it away without having touched the display.

Then she closed the app.

Images of Older Women

(The performer strikes the poses
and make the gestures.)

Older woman who is lying on her back on the floor looking at the stars.

Older woman who is hammering a nail into the parquet floor.

Older woman on all fours, looking into the grass.

Older woman who is walking across the stage as if she were pulling a rolling suitcase behind her.

Older woman who is looking at her fingernails with abhorrence.

Older woman who is hugging herself.

Older woman who was just hit by a shot.

Older woman who is holding up a little dog, cuddling him.

Older woman who is throwing herself backwards onto a bed (ten times in a row).

Older woman who wakes up in the morning, squints into the light (the light comes from an asteroid strike a bit further away, so that it doesn't hit the woman directly, but the dust and darkness will descend on her soon).

ELEVEN

Hey gnome.
I've missed you.
And your face too.

When exactly did Benu write this? Juno didn't know any more. She needed all of her strength not to let his next sentences get to her.

They kept coming back to her.

Sometimes, Juno thought they were very sweet.

She had written to Benu several times, telling him that he should stop.

That she thought it undignified. He should never again write that he was in love with her.

He wrote that he didn't think anything of it and that he didn't have any ulterior motives. It was just what he was feeling.

He didn't want to harass her. But he wanted to tell her anyway.

That you should take life lightly, but that it was important to always be honest.

I am. Definitely.

Nevertheless, Juno couldn't bring herself to block the

WhatsApp contact and report him. It would have taken just two clicks, then ciao for ever.

Ciao for ever?

Benu had her number; he would be able to write to her again using a new profile.

Would you do something like that, Benu? *If I want to, I can simply delete you.*

And I you.

It sounded like something from a novel.

The plot: woman answers scammer, scammer falls in love, she is annoyed, doesn't believe in anything like love, barks at him, he doesn't let go.

The ex-scammer smuggles himself on a ship to Europe, makes it to Chemnitz, is standing in front of her door one morning, and THE END.

But this here was reality. She didn't live in Chemnitz.

She lived with Jupiter in an apartment with glass doors.

Reality was brutal.

Reality was also that Jupiter still didn't know anything about Benu.

Hey, Jupi, by the way, I've been chatting with a love scammer for four months.

Hey, Jupi, somehow it's the only secret that remains for me between all of the glass doors here in the apartment.

Hey, Jupi, that's right, it's kind of an adventure and I know I'm behaving no better than the husbands over fifty who cheat on their wives. The set-up is the same, even though this isn't about desire.

I know, I'm engaging in a social behaviour that I always found intolerable.

Jupi would have understood all this.

But Juno couldn't bring herself to tell him.
And she was surprised that Benu just kept writing to her.
How stubborn he was.
Undeterred, he kept sending his sentences over.

> Your new haircut is cute.
> I like the shape of your head!

No one had ever said that to her before. Juno had never thought about the shape of her head. And she had cut her hair herself, as always, after a hairdresser had cut her an exaggeratedly precise pageboy the day before. She went home and, in the bathroom, took a pair of household scissors and cut right across the strands, making a jagged fringe. Something between semi-long and short.
In order to look less normal again.

> Aha.

> Are you mad again?
> What's so bad about paying
> you a compliment?

The next morning, she sent Benu a voice memo.
Hey Benu, she began.
That she had already said it a thousand times.
Benu and she, two normal people, were here on the Earth in two far-apart places and were talking. Full stop. Nothing more.
Without romantic stuff, do you understand?
Without this stuff about being in love.
Eye-to-eye, etc., with no flirtation.
I'm not interested in that, and I never was.

And then she said for fun, and she laughed while she was speaking, and to Juno it was clear that she was making a joke – what kind of stupid joke was that?

Later, Juno thought that she had said it without enough consideration. She said as a joke:

And if you don't stop and you tell me again that you've fallen in love with me, you should drop dead on the spot.

Juno said that she knew something about witchcraft.

I'm into witchcraft, you know.

That came to her out of the blue; she was reading a volume of poetry, *Witch*.

Poems that played with witchcraft and the devil.

Black magic and sex between devils and witches.

The poems were serious and not serious at the same time, by a wonderful woman poet from England.

Nobody in Germany would trust themselves to write something like that, Juno thought at the time.

Otherwise, she wasn't interested in witchcraft as a topic, she found it too esoteric, ridiculous when women met on *Walpurgisnacht* for dance parties and things like that.

'Witch' was what one of the boys in elementary school called her.

Witch was something Salvan had said to her once. She was ugly like a witch.

There were good reasons not to flirt with the topic.

There was no message all day.

Only in the evening.

Tell me, is it true that you know a bit
about witchcraft?

No, that's nonsense, it was just a joke
I don't believe in witches, they don't
interest me at all, I like spirits and devils,
but only in art.

It's good to believe in all that.
Do you remember, the Wilis in Giselle
and such?

You shouldn't joke about this, neither about
witches nor about spirits.
I implore you not to say the word witch or write it
to me.
I'm very scared.
The word frightens me.

Something in what he wrote was an alarm.
Something in his voice was running away.
Something in the message was, Juno knew, actually true and
meant seriously this time.

Okay. Sorry, I didn't mean to do that.
It was really only a joke.
Of course I have nothing to do with
witchcraft.
Okay, thank you.
There aren't actually any witches, are there?

No response.

In the apartment it was so still that the sleeping birds in
the trees outside sounded loud.

What was he talking about, witches? Witches were the
women in fairy tales who were always evil.

They didn't interest her.

And if anything did, then it was spirits. Perhaps the wild bee outside on the balcony had been a spirit.

★ ★ ★

In Germany, there was a tidal wave of witches in the theatres. Performances about witchcraft, witch dances, witch fires.

Juno had almost argued with a colleague once. She found it unpleasant when historic, brutal facts were neglected, Juno said to the colleague, and that in the theatres only the fairy-tale element came to light, the usual images of smoke, women's secret knowledge, the non-conformist witches.

People were working with old stereotypes but trying to turn them to the good.

To party like witches.

Yet there was no witchcraft, only thousands of women who were brutally killed.

Perhaps someone should write a theatre piece about that, if anything.

★ ★ ★

Only much later did Juno happen to read a newspaper article about the belief in witches in West African countries.

That it came from the many free church Christian movements that were overrunning the country, mixed with the remains of old religions.

There were people, especially in the countryside, who were called witches, arbitrarily, and banned from the villages. Even children.

As well as that, there were so-called healers who took in these children. The children had to work for the healers and the healers promised the parents that they would rid their children of the devil.

Some of them never saw their parents again.

One of the documentaries on YouTube had shown a love scammer in Ghana on his way to the 'Voodoo' priest. 'Voodoo' in quotation marks.

You saw the man walking on red tar streets. He had a printed-out photo of a woman in his hand. This was a woman who didn't want to transfer any money. Not yet.

The 'Voodoo' priest killed a goat in the courtyard of his house, a beautiful white goat with bent horns. The scammer had to pour the goat's blood over a bundle a little later. It was called 'spirit' in the documentary.

It was the goat's rump, without a head, without legs.

The scammer had to tie the bundle with a cord, there were precise instructions for how to make the knots. Then the scammer lifted up the bundle, threw it on the ground with all his might, the priest lit a fire and sparks sprayed from it.

The sparks would blind the victim, said the priest, the woman who didn't want to transfer money. Not yet. A person who was blinded would do everything that you asked him or her to do.

As soon as the woman transferred money to the love scammer, the priest would get a share.

'Voodoo' was not the right word; that was something the people in the documentary should have found out. The documentary was on Spiegel TV, what else would you expect?

'Voodoo' was and is an invention of the Western world.

'Voodoo' was at the most this film with Mickey Rourke; Juno had forgotten the title, it was set in New Orleans, there was chicken blood and death and sex. The film had annoyed Juno because suddenly her friends wanted to be like Mickey Rourke, and hearts were ripped out of bodies and the devil played a part too.

The correct term was Voudou. Sometimes also Vodun or Vodoun.

Juno had googled it during the documentary.

It was a monotheistic religion, not one that only worshipped spirits, as everyone said. It was a religion, after all.

Un-ideal, like all religions.

At the time, Juno didn't know what was worse, the poorly researched documentary or the thing with the poor goat or that people wanted to put a spell on the poor woman who didn't want to pay.

★ ★ ★

Juno closed her laptop.

There were a lot of documentaries in the meantime, ones she had watched since she met Benu. They didn't make what was happening on Earth any clearer, they only showed how interwoven and inextricable everything was.

In the documentary, the same scammer who went to the priest had also said that what he was doing was okay. The older women he was deceiving were the heirs of the colonial power of Europe over Africa. Someone had to pay for this.

Juno thought he was making things too easy for himself.

Juno opened her laptop again. She made a note: 'Soft war' as a title for her theatre piece. Two marginalized groups facing off. They were not fighting one another, that was the wrong word. They were wrestling with one another.

Her phone rang. The pearly tone.

Benu's face jumped into the picture. He looked curious, inquisitive.

Juno tried again not to smile.

A candle was lit in a nice room in a medium-sized city in Nigeria while the smaller Leipzig sent its power unperturbed through the lines and lit up its streets and houses until early morning. There were no documentaries about that.

Juno had the energy-saving lamp on.

Sorry, said Benu. I'm sorry about the thing with the witch.

No problem, said Juno.

Then Benu said that he had actually thought at one point that she might be something like a witch.

I couldn't see how old you are, he said. Who you are. Sometimes I had the feeling that you're just playing with me, he said.

Juno had a bad conscience.

He actually didn't believe in witches, said Benu then.

In the village where his aunts live, many people believe in witches. Most of the time he thought it was silly, but then it was hard to extract yourself from it. It was said that witches brought hunger. They made animals sick, made the fields dry out.

Of course there are rational explanations for why the animals get sick, said Benu. But the irrational explanations are easier.

He kept pausing between sentences and individual words in order to say everything with special emphasis.

And sometimes there are those moments where you think maybe there's something to all that.

I'm familiar with that, said Juno. She thought about how sometimes she was still convinced that Benu was only interested in the money she didn't have.

Or how sometimes she considered whether Jupiter's illness was an evil fate. Many people believe that Jupiter's illness is inherited, it's due to his genes. And yet that wasn't right. But what if it was right? Jupiter's mother also suffered from this illness and, in the end, died in a nursing home.

Maybe that's why Benu sometimes called very early in the morning, via video call. Often her phone rang at 4 a.m.

Maybe Benu wanted to see whether she had just returned from her witches' night out and there were signs: wide-open eyes, tousled hair. Juno had no idea what a modern witch might look like. Hi, she said each time; she saw herself in the lower right corner of the screen on the phone, wide awake, as always.

Sleeplessness was like a spell. Or was it a curse?

You told me that your mother brought in a spirit healer when your father lay dying. So don't tell me that this is completely ridiculous.

Benu smiled as he said that, and it seemed to Juno that he suspected what she had just been thinking.

If you had an invisible friend who was always with you when you were a child, perhaps that's a similar kind of thing, responded Juno. You know that the friend is not real, but when you imagine him, he's still very real. And you feel good that you're not alone.

So, there's no difference between a real and an imaginary friend? said Benu.

A real friend pulls you back if you nearly step off the

pavement in front of a car because you're not paying attention. An imaginary friend doesn't.

As soon as she'd said this, she noticed that it sounded like a subtle hint that Benu had first written to her as a love scammer. And she hadn't meant it that way.

They were both silent for a moment. They looked at each other, then they started to laugh.

Oh man, said Benu, still grinning broadly. Real deep talk.

But let's go back to the witch thing, said Juno then.

I'm the most normal person in the world. I have zero interest in magic and things like that.

That she was only slightly quirky. She couldn't think of the English word for quirky right away.

When you're a little crazy, you know?

Quirky, said Benu.

Exactly. But something physical. Like a little disability. Like if you're in a wheelchair, but different.

Benu was grinning again.

Aha, I get it.

Outside, coincidentally, there was a full moon. She stood with her back to the window and saw that you could see the moon on the display. Quickly, she walked away from the window. Not the full moon too. Somehow, they ended the video call. Later on, Juno could not remember exactly what they said. In any case, not much more.

But Benu put a hand to his mouth; that much she could remember. He kissed his fingertips, then he held them up to the camera, towards Juno.

He made another serious face.

At once his eyes were sad, Juno thought that.

TWELVE

Juno Isabella Flock cut her own hair at the age of ten, with small golden scissors from her mother's sewing basket. More and more often, she also cut parts of her clothing, removing the hems on the sleeves or the feet of the stockings that she had to wear in the winter. Sometimes, she just made long slits in the legs of her trousers.

So that it's airier, she told her mother.

At first her parents were in uproar about this, but at some point they accepted it.

At school, she spent most of her time during the breaks by herself.

Well, your name is Juno, she heard a girl from her class whispering to the girl who sat next to her.

Once, her mother took Juno to a doctor.

An older, friendly man with horn-rimmed glasses. He smoked a cigar while he was asking Juno questions, all of which her mother answered. The doctor wrote a prescription for a packet of tablets. To calm her. And he told Juno's mother Juno should eat toasted oats for breakfast; they were good for the nerves and tasted good too.

She had to take the tablets after breakfast. Juno held them in her cheek until she was out of the house. She spat them out on the gravel on the driveway and didn't even bother to use her toes to spread gravel over the tablets.

The toasted oats for breakfast tasted okay, but even after four years, it hadn't cured her.

At some point, Nyx came into her life. That wasn't a cure either, but Nyx didn't care about Juno's hair and the cut-up hems and sleeves; he even liked them. Cuts everywhere in her clothes, in her hair. Sometimes, Juno sewed the cuts up again, with crooked, intentionally poor stitches. She liked that. She also liked her hair. Meanwhile, the first punks had appeared in the large cities and at school, everyone thought Juno was one of those.

She had always been *strange*.

Had looked strange, stood there strangely, said strange things.

She wasn't allowed a part in any of the school plays. And she didn't want one either.

Then came the issue with her spatial understanding, it also wasn't so bad. Then came all of her special interests. Space. Juno borrowed a lot of books from the town library. Furthermore, all the books about ballet. Instantly, she could name the ballet in which Louis XIV, the Sun King, had played the main role: *Le Ballet Royal de la Nuit*. The king played the rising sun.

That's the original of the name Sun King, she said once in school to her history teacher, ninth grade, absolutism. She simply interrupted him and talked about the king's passion for dance. The others in her class laughed; they thought she was doing it as some kind of class clown, but she was completely serious.

Her parents spoke to Juno less and less. Sometimes, it seemed they were afraid of her. Increasingly they were occupied only with themselves; her father mowed the grass for hours, forgetting everything around him and marching along stoically behind the lawnmower. Her mother did the same thing with the vacuum cleaner, and in the evenings cooked large steaming dishes, pouring spaghetti into giant pots with boiling water and stirring the Bolognese sauce in the pan. Then they sat at the table for over an hour and were occupied with their meal. Every evening, Juno took her plate into her room.

Once, she heard a woman from the village say to her grandmother, who lived a few streets away: *Your granddaughter has fallen victim to a demon.*

At some point, Juno packed a backpack and moved into the house of a woman who lived far out in the valley.

The thing with the treehouse, Aamon and Salvan was as good as history by then. That incident wasn't anything that made anything else worse. They didn't have that much power. The house stood at the foot of a mountain, right next to the gravel bank of the Vils, the river that flowed through the village with its swirling, hopping rapids.

There was a home-made sign on the garden fence: room available for help in the house and in the barn.

The woman kept a small herd of five sheep, plus a dozen chickens in a barn behind the house, but only as a hobby.

She seemed to be rich, although the rooms in the house were simple, old furniture and no great luxury. The woman published books.

Later, Juno couldn't even say what kind of books; she just remembered a few book spines with the woman's name on them on a shelf, and that the woman sat in her office and typed on a typewriter until late in the evening, smoking.

She always had kohl around her eyes, and she wore crocheted black dresses.

In the town, some people said she was 'a crazy woman'.

She had moved to the town as a young woman, before Juno was born, she told Juno.

Juno helped with the sheep and chickens.

It was nice to shoo the chickens into the chicken coop with big arm movements.

Juno enjoyed the feeling of tiny power that she had over the chickens, who followed her everywhere for a few grains of corn. But she also loved the chickens because they trusted her so innocently.

It was nice when the five sheep greeted her with their multi-voiced bleating in the barn.

Juno cleaned the house, vacuumed, mopped the floors and washed the dishes. The house wasn't especially dirty.

It seemed to be a good solution for everyone.

How old was Juno? Sixteen.

The writing woman had a sewing machine that Juno was allowed to use, and in the living room there was a giant chest with fabric remnants.

Go on, said the woman to her, and left the room, smoking. Sometimes Juno appeared in town to go shopping with dresses she had sewn herself and her self-cut hair, and she saw how people in cars turned their heads and looked at her.

That looks good, said Nyx. Nyx was still there; his hair had long since grown back.

We have to get used to the thought that nothing is for ever, Juno said to him at some point. And first Nyx cried briefly, then he nodded. A little while later, he moved to live with his father in Brittany.

At some point, other girls from the village came to Juno on the farm and asked her to cut their hair.

At some point, she also sewed dresses for them.

At some point, she asked them for money for doing this.

The less she could tolerate the girls who came to her –

they were pretty and blonde and played tennis at the tennis club and went to the big, new discotheques nearby out in the green fields outside the city. Juno knew that they thought she was strange, but her clothes had that special style, something that wasn't available anywhere except in London; that's why they were forced to come to Juno on the edge of town –

the more money she asked them for.

The girls always paid, even if Juno suddenly raised her prices arbitrarily.

Juno thought life was half okay. But only half.

Fallen victim to a demon?

There were at least a hundred.

★ ★ ★

Jupiter's toothache didn't go away.

It got worse, the ibuprofen bottles piled up.

When Jupiter wanted to chew on the side of that tooth – it was the first molar on the lower right next to the canine – spikes of pain shot across half of his face.

He couldn't sleep at night, but he didn't call for Juno.

Juno only noticed because she was just as awake as he was.

She saw the bluish light streaming from his room, as if it were carrying the toothache outside, over to her, into the room with the planets.

Or it was carrying only the pain, without the tooth.

Several times in the evening she went over, asked if Jupiter needed anything, then he said: No, everything's okay; it's getting better.

Then each morning, it actually was better and Jupiter put off the plan to go to the dentist's office again.

The pain would probably go away.

It had already almost gone away.

The rehearsals for the guest performances in Munich began in a week; it was an event in the future.

Juno said it would be better to go to the dentist now so that everything would be okay when she was in Munich.

On the fourth day, however, the pain went away in the evening, as if miraculously.

Everything in Jupiter's face was once again light and straight.

Juno brought him two raisin buns with butter in bed. First Jupi chewed them carefully, then more courageously; he was doing better, everything would be okay, as always. They had made it this far, they would continue to make it, but how exactly?

Juno took the tram into the city; she wanted to go to TK Maxx because they always had cheap, crazy clothing, jumpers with sequins and trousers in garish colours.

They wanted new costumes for the performances in Munich; Phoebus and Tristan had already found something.

Juno hadn't decided yet, there would be something, a shiny top, neon leggings, maybe bright pink socks.

The tram was full, and it rumbled. Juno sat in a seat directly behind the entrance, a stop, the doors slid open, letting in a wave of cold. It was raining outside. Leipzig slid by, still stony grey, still lit up in its nineteenth-century houses.

Four ticket inspectors got on, portly men who had fastened visible identification cards in plastic sleeves on their jackets.

First, they checked the ticket of a veiled woman standing next to a pushchair; in it, a small child, who looked on curiously.

The woman took a monthly pass out of a bag and showed it to the ticket inspectors. They took the pass out of her hand, turned it over several times, and read everything written on it thoroughly and with sceptical expressions before holding the pass up to their reader.

Juno had the same pass. There was much less to read on it than the time the men spent doing so warranted.

Two dark-skinned young men boarded the car, and the ticket inspectors went right to them and demanded their tickets.

There were several people standing between them and the veiled woman; actually, they should have been the next ones to show their tickets.

A woman with a big white dog had boarded, a guide dog with a special harness.

The woman was wearing glasses and held her head straight. She moved with such certainty that you could see she couldn't see anything.

The seat next to Juno was empty, the dog seemed to notice this and led the woman right to it.

The dog looked at Juno with a brief, serious look before he moved aside and made way for the woman, who sat down next to Juno without hesitation.

The woman was tall and took up more than half the bench. Juno could feel her upper arms.

You have good posture, said the woman to Juno at some point, and Juno was a little startled. Because the sentence came from out of the blue and it was unusual for a woman who clearly couldn't see anything.

And you have pretty shoes.

Can you sense that somehow? asked Juno, and she noticed how dumb the sentence was. She saw that the dog was following her words attentively; he tilted his head.

No, said the woman, I can see that; I still have 10 per cent.

Excuse me, said Juno, and she was ashamed, but the woman, who was still young (probably not even thirty), turned her face towards her. Juno had the feeling that she was scanning Juno's face with her eyes behind the sunglasses.

You don't have to be ashamed, she said. Everyone feels that way when they talk to me.

The woman seemed to be a clairvoyant; Juno didn't like that thought, but it shot through her head.

Now the ticket inspectors came to them too, Juno showed them her pass. Without even looking, the woman pulled a disabled identification card out of her handbag, which seemed to be full to the brim. Juno was familiar with this identification card because of Jupiter. There was another part in the sleeve that showed that you were allowed to ride for free. But for this, you had to pay an annual fee to the city.

This time too, the ticket inspectors took the woman's pass and examined it in detail. As if they were expecting all of this to be falsified, the identification card, the dog, the glasses, the visual disability.

That also happened to Jupiter often when he was checked. At some point his disabled identification card was turned and turned again.

When the ticket inspectors were gone, they sat in silence for a while.

Then Juno heard the echoing ping of WhatsApp from her bumbag.

Probably Benu.

Your lover is texting you. I can hear that from the tone, said the woman, and Juno was startled again, for in a certain sense, she was right. But the woman laughed right after that; it was just a joke, she said. That's my favourite joke when the topic is my eyes.

Juno said: Aha, and laughed too.

The tram reached the Goerdelerring and Juno was a bit relieved that she could get off.

Take care, said the woman, when Juno stood up.

Juno said, Of course, you too.

The dog looked alertly through the carriage. A lot of people wanted to get off, there was a little crowd in front of the doors. For a moment, Juno had the urge to pet the dog, but she knew that you weren't allowed to do that with service dogs. They had to keep their work and private lives separate. When Juno was outside on the platform, she saw that the woman was waving to her from the departing tram.

She turned her head towards Juno, precisely in her direction.

★ ★ ★

At night, she found Jupiter stretched out on the floor in his room.

Jupiter in his layers of gas and fog.

Juno, the space probe, which had been shot up to Jupiter so that she could record everything about him.

Jupiter's eye is a whirlwind that has lasted at least two hundred years, the largest one in the solar system.

Jupiter had called her that night; Juno didn't hear it right away, even though she was still awake. She was lying on the floor next to the Pilates ball; she was holding it between her thighs and doing sit-ups this way, so that the inner muscles of her thighs got a workout too. Those muscles were critical for ballet.

Then she was relaxing and Benu had called.

She had refused the call and messaged him to say that she had to take a break. Things couldn't go on this way.

Like with a couple that had fought.

And then she heard Jupiter calling.

He was lying in his room stretched out on the floor and he couldn't get up. His knees were much stiffer than usual.

He had tried to get up and support himself on the walker in order to get ibuprofen from the little cabinet in the hall.

And then he had just tipped over, his legs went out from under him.

Probably an episode, said Jupiter.

Juno was familiar with these; particular infections in the body – the teeth, the tonsils, the bladder – caused episodes, some kind of overflow of the defences.

Some kind of chaos, particles shooting around the body, cutting all the lines.

They decided to call the emergency doctor.

Juno had learned to ignore the shock that she felt when she saw Jupiter lying on the floor and to put herself into a semi-practical mode. Although sometimes it was an aimless act. She went into the kitchen even though she didn't know what she should do there, perhaps get a glass of water, then back, put a blanket over Jupiter so that he wasn't cold.

During the first episode fifteen years ago, nobody knew that it was an episode. The emergency doctor they called had a beer belly and stood snuffling in Jupiter's room and had asked whether Jupiter had taken drugs.

Juno got out her phone and tried to explain to the dispatcher calmly and coolly what was happening. Even so, her voice had a desperate undertone.

She rode along in the ambulance to the hospital even though Jupiter didn't want her to.

I can do this alone, he said; you know how things are in the emergency room.

It was not the first episode; the last two times, Juno hadn't gone along. But this time she did. She wouldn't have been able to sleep anyway.

There were a lot of drunk people in the room to which the sick and injured were brought first. At least the ones who didn't seem to be severely injured.

There was an initial brief examination by a young doctor with dark circles under his eyes, then Juno was sent out; they had to perform the normal examinations.

She sat on a bench in the foyer, got one coffee after another from the machine, tired light from long tubes fell across the hall, only a few people other than her who, like her, were waiting for someone.

They were afraid or hopeful or perhaps they didn't feel anything at all.

Later, she left St George via the main entrance. She paused briefly under the awning; the grounds were still asleep.

It was already about 2 a.m.

The young doctor with the dark circles under his eyes had come to see her in the room. Jupiter would have to stay in. He would be admitted to the neurology department. They would have to investigate what in Jupiter's body had been damaged irreparably this time.

She was allowed into the room briefly, where Jupiter was lying on a bed, surrounded by drunken people who were nagging or babbling.

This was familiar.

Go on home, said Jupi.

Tomorrow, she had a rehearsal for the guest performances in Munich, until 3 p.m.

It would be okay if she came by after that, said Jupiter, to bring him his things.

Of course it would be okay.

You can't do much here anyway, said Jupiter.

Meanwhile, Juno knew this too, it wasn't the first episode.

She went out into the clear air; it was quiet, the sick and injured long since sleeping in their beds, or at least quiet.

She had called a taxi, the tram had stopped running at that hour. It would cost at least thirty euros to take her from this end of the city back to her neighbourhood.

Juno stood under the awning and thought how nice this moment was.

Just the moment, nothing around it, not the situation, just standing and waiting in the still night, and at that exact moment there were flickers in the night-orange sky.

Pulsating flickers of light, which came from above and lit up the sky again and again. At first, Juno thought it might be a thunderstorm, but the sky was cloudless, and it was April.

Then a thunderous noise flooded the air.

It was the rescue helicopter, taking off from the roof above her.

Then the wind from the rotor blades started.

The strange thing was that this wind didn't reach her under the awning of the foyer; her hair wasn't disturbed and didn't fly around, and she couldn't feel it in her face.

But the wind was visible. There were lots of trees on the grounds, their tops waved back and forth, and you could hear the blades rushing.

Juno stayed still. How nice this moment was, and how happy she was to have experienced it, a valuable moment of true beauty.

For it was beauty that remained in memory in the end. Not external beauty, but the beauty of a moment that was completely insignificant.

Now the noise was so loud that Juno had to hold her hands over her ears. And then she saw the helicopter; it flew briefly over the grounds, turned in a sharp curve and flew away. You could hear its rattling for a long while.

Somewhere, someone was having an emergency. Juno wished this person well.

She wished everyone well.

All of the people around her who needed help, all the best.

Jupiter, Benu.

Cielo, who had taken her hands in his and needed a place to sleep. The men who wrote to her saying that she was an interesting artist and had a nice figure. Grey-haired Pluto, who wanted to have her e-mail address and had received a story about her job in the observatory in Schkeuditz.

The love scammers to whom she had lied so badly.

All the best to all of you.

★ ★ ★

At the rehearsal the next day, at first, she didn't tell Phoebus and Tristan anything about Jupiter's episode. Why should she? In the meantime, all of this was so routine that she could handle it.

She spoke her lines into the microphone as always, her voice sounded good, said Phoebus later. Juno was happy. That's it, that's why you live, for happiness.

After the rehearsal, she took the number sixteen tram back to the hospital, brought Jupiter three T-shirts, two pairs of trousers and underwear, his toothbrush, a few books and his laptop.

Just don't fall into despair now, keep on going, don't stray from the path. Follow fixed plans, schedules, rehearsal plans and times.

How long would things continue to go well?

Juno spent the whole evening with Jupiter; luckily the other bed in the room was not occupied and they had some peace and quiet.

They played a few rounds of gin rummy and watched *Heute* together, then Jupiter was tired. She rode home on the number sixteen tram at about 8 p.m.

Change at the main train station, the line one to her neighbourhood was not running, an accident, the line was blocked –

sometimes everything that could went wrong, all at once –

and 14 September, which was yet to come, was still a long way off. That day on which Juno wanted to buy the spiced Christmas biscuits in the supermarket and heard the young woman say that old people who bought Christmas goodies in September had only themselves to blame. That day, when she stood crying between the aisles because she didn't know what else she should buy, or not buy, so that Jupiter would survive on the one hand, but also the world on the other. She, Juno, thought that she was somehow the pivot around which everything revolved, that other people's lives intersected in her, and that she was responsible for how those lives turned out.

Who should be able to withstand all this? Juno would think on 14 September, and sink down crying on the floor of the Leipzig supermarket, where there was nobody to help her up again.

Everyone just looked down at her strangely. At some point she managed to stand up again, and only then did the supermarket manager come over, a woman of her age with yellow-blonde hair and a burgundy and white striped jumper, who asked: Is everything okay?

And Juno said, Thank you, yes, everything's okay, but she just found out that her cat had been run over by a car.

But it's okay, said Juno, really. Thank you very much, thank you. And she took her purchases home.

★ ★ ★

And now we see Juno Isabella Flock boarding tram line three, to the *Adler*; the evening isn't over yet.

At the *Adler*, finally on line one, which will take her to her stop from the other direction.

The tram is still stopped. Juno jumps on and goes down the aisle towards the back. It's empty in most of the carriages; it's an XXL-liner, you can see all the way to the back; an elderly couple is sitting a few rows further back.

Outside on the platform, four boys, barely thirteen, are fooling around a bit, nothing notable.

It's warm in the tram, the heaters are hissing.

Suddenly, a few dull thuds, the boys outside are hitting the window, there, where the couple is sitting, bam, bam, bam. They're making faces, not funny ones, but evil, distorted faces.

And there, now one of them has spat on the window, just where the woman is sitting.

The woman jerks back, her husband cries: Are you crazy? Although the boys outside can't hear him.

The whole thing happens so fast that Juno perceives it with a slight delay. She's just sitting there, on a seat next to the window, the tram is still stopped.

And suddenly the boys are next to her.

Very near the window, grimacing, and again, bam, bam, bam.

One of the three bangs the window angrily; Juno thinks it will break.

And then one of the boys spits at her too. Presses a load of spit against his lips with all his might.

It's not the window that he's aiming to hit.

Why is he doing that? thinks Juno.

Does she look as *strange* as before?

Can he just spit at her like that?

Right next to her cheek, foamy spit runs down the glass.

And she looks at the one who spat through the thin window, which lets all the evil energy in.

He has a hollowed-out face like that of an older man, almost translucent, this white skin, you can see blue veins at his temples.

There actually are people like that. She had thought that before. Once again, she had to think about Aamon and Salvan. Who apparently always carried scissors.

Those could be their spirits on the platform.

She feels her stony grey gaze meet the boy's ice-blue gaze for a long while.

She notes how her gaze hits the boy like the tip of a needle.

For a moment, there's a hint of wonder in his face. He pauses, just like the love scammers pause.

Does she really mean that? Oh, she really means it, he wants to shift his gaze, but it gets caught again.

And they hold out, hold out, hold out.

The tram departs, Juno holds his gaze, holds it, holds; the boy holds it too, holds it too. There's a silence and a cold current between them, and Juno thinks that she's in the process of sending him a curse.

An evil curse that damages everything, nature, his heart.

Benu, I'm still not a witch.

Once again, brief amazement in the boy's gaze.

Juno thinks that he somehow suspects that she's cursing him, but she can't see whether he's frightened.

Whether it's hurting him.

Then the tram turns the corner and they're gone.

One of them was the devil; that feeling was present the whole time, just like this evil energy, Juno doesn't know from whom or what it emanates.

It doesn't matter whether something really exists or whether you just imagine it strongly enough, didn't Benu say that recently?

The older couple is still fussing. A thing like that, such a rabble.

Perhaps three minutes have passed. Light travels a distance of 33.5 million miles in this time.

How insignificant these three minutes with the boys at the window are in the end, thinks Juno. You can confidently let them slide into oblivion.

THIRTEEN

It's the end of April already.

Time is no longer like a line but rather more like a soup.

Only the fact that we are getting closer to death looms in each action, in each event.

Regardless of what you're doing,

watering the flowers,

eating a piece of bread,

you're doing it on the way to death.

This process is called ageing.

You start ageing from the day you are born.

★ ★ ★

At night, Juno saw through the glass door into Jupiter's room; the blue shimmer of his display was missing.

Sometimes, she noticed how different it was in the apartment. Just her, alone there. Still quieter, of course. Nothing moved behind the glass doors. Juno thought about how rarely this happened. And that it could also be nice to be alone in the apartment.

That was something that she did not allow herself to think.

Being alone for a longer period of time in an apartment, Juno no longer knew how that felt. Going from your room into the kitchen and making tea without anyone watching you.

Day three after Jupiter's episode, Juno had not had time to visit, so they spoke on the phone.

How are you doing? What did they find in the examinations?

Nothing really new there, but the tests weren't complete yet.

Okay, shit, but perhaps you'll get out the day after tomorrow?

Let's see, said Jupiter, I don't think so. I'm still not steady on my legs.

I think an earwig has moved into the insect hotel, said Juno.

She had seen a small, longish body flit into one of the tubes when she went out on the balcony briefly in the afternoon to shake out her bedclothes.

I was always afraid of earwigs as a child, said Jupiter. People told us that they creep into your ear when you're sleeping and then you would get sick.

Same here, said Juno.

Maybe that's right, said Jupiter, and I once got an earwig like that.

Oh you, said Juno.

They said goodbye.

Ciao, talk to you tomorrow. Sleep well.

Juno fell into bed.

She actually wanted to sleep. Because tomorrow she would have to go back to the daily grind so that they would have enough to eat next week.

When Jupi came home again.

She had to clean the bathroom and maybe put clean sheets on the bed, etc.

★ ★ ★

Of course, right after that, another love scammer sent her a message. Juno had surreptitiously checked under 'Requests' on Instagram. It was a habit that you didn't engage in consciously, like chewing your fingernails.

Hi, victim.

Samuel_Webster.

Be good was the slogan in his profile, a white, smiling man with glasses and a light-coloured baseball cap.

Three posts. 77 followers. 657 following.

Always the same old story.

Hi.

What was Juno doing?

> I'm sitting in my room, that much
> is true.
> Be good, what a nice slogan.
> Are you a good person?
> Why are you lying?
> Should I tell you a true story?
> One of you love scammers says
> that he loves me and that he thinks
> I'm a witch.
> And also, my husband is in the hospital.
> That's all.

Juno was blocked.

FOURTEEN

And then he was gone. Benu was gone.

Juno could still see his profile on WhatsApp, but the photo had disappeared.

Now there was a white shadowy figure in a grey circle.

She typed 'hey' into the chat box, and only a grey tick appeared. It became two grey ticks.

Benu had become a ghost. He was somewhere in the grey nothingness.

Ursa Minor stood vertically in the sky over Benu's city, Juno could see that on timeanddate.com. She had opened the page and entered the name of the city, then up sprang the night sky that Benu could see above him now if the weather was good.

Right now she wanted to see the sky over Benu's city in real-time animation. As if she could find Benu there. Further to the north was Ursa Major, directly above that the hunting dogs, and a bit further to the west the lion, this time standing on his head.

Juno didn't dare to type anything into the speech bubble again. What's going on? Where have you gone?

There would be two more ticks, which would turn blue.

She looked briefly out the window.

Melancholia had just disappeared; Juno did not know

where it had gone, but it wasn't there at that moment. Actually, it hadn't been there for a while.

Actually, the last few weeks had been okay in a strange way, and she had only seldom listened to the film score. Perhaps because so much was going on.

In the early evening, she had talked to Jupiter on the phone; a day ago, he had been transferred to a rehab clinic near Leipzig.

It's brilliant, said Jupiter, truly luxurious. I even have a single room because the shared rooms are all full.

Three weeks of massages, poultices and physiotherapy.

Not bad, said Juno.

If she took the train, she could be there in twenty minutes. There was also a public thermal bath nearby. After visiting Jupiter, she could always go swimming and laze on a lounger a little, in pleasantly tempered air that felt subtropical, without having to forgo the comfort and advantages of their temperate climate zone.

And Jupiter's novel would be published next spring, by a big publisher. The agency to which he had given his manuscript had called him in the rehab clinic. There would be a not-so-small advance. We're rich, said Jupiter into the telephone, and they laughed again.

We'll use the money to open a luxury insect hotel, said Juno. Then the wild bees will be breaking down our doors.

★ ★ ★

One more day until the performance in Munich.

Is it really okay if I go? she asked Jupiter on the telephone.

Do you think I'll actually get well if you don't go? asked Jupiter in return.

There was a brief, indecisive pause because Juno didn't know whether there had been a subtle, cynical undertone to Jupiter's question.

As if I could have anything against a performance, said Jupiter then. It would be like asking you not to breathe any more.

Of course that's right, if you look at it that way, said Juno, and Jupiter laughed.

Tristan and Phoebus had found a driver, everything was packed, the costumes were in their bags. She knew her lines, she knew the dance movements. She was over fifty; perhaps it would matter to her that the people in the audience might look at her strangely but now was not the time to think about that.

The theatre in Munich had also had posters printed, once again the ones with Juno, Phoebus and Tristan in the decommissioned fountain.

The woman handling the publicity had sent Juno photos.

The posters were now hanging everywhere in Munich. Perhaps there would be more cities too.

The car would be outside her door at 8 a.m. tomorrow.

She would have liked to tell Benu about this. She would have been able to send him a few photos. Perhaps she would have told him the truth soon. The whole truth.

She typed into the speech bubble again. As if Benu were still there, and he was too.

He was somewhere out there. If she just imagined hard enough that he was reading what she was writing, then it would be okay. Then he would read it.

Hey Benu, how are you doing?
When you read this, the planet
Melancholia will long since
have been swallowed by a black hole.
What's going on, where have you gone?
It could be that you don't want to write
to me any more and that's okay.
Maybe you were messaging me as a
scammer the whole time,
I will never know.
But I'll stick to what I actually know.

I'm doing well. A lot is going on here.
I have decided to go to bed earlier.
Have you watched the film since we
spoke?
I will never be able to decide who I
would rather be, Claire or Justine.
Each is strong in her own way and yet
neither of them survive but they have
each other.
Maybe I'm like both of them.
And in the end, I have only myself.

Perhaps I also had you for a while.

I have thought about friendship, for the
first time in my life.
Perhaps we were something like that:
friends.
Or we could have been friends.
I would have liked to have you as a
friend.

We'll see each other again, in another
life, in another world.
Be well, for always, your Juno.

A grey tick.
The main thing is that the message was sent.

FIFTEEN

And then it was May.

Juno stepped into the ballet studio and suddenly the Earth was beautiful and bright.

Suddenly the ballet studio was a little box where life played out, only this one, special life that you have.

In this life, Juno danced the position in the *Pas de Quatre* that nobody other than Marie Taglioni danced at the premiere in 1845.

During the rehearsals, she wore fine little sleeves of white tulle on her upper arms; they were supposed to represent fairy wings.

That was part of the costume.

She was doing much better. She was sleeping, actually sleeping, and the dogs from her dreams had disappeared.

Jupiter was also doing better; he was at home and could sit in his wheelchair for a longer time again and even move pretty well through the apartment with his walker. He didn't have to lie down so much any more.

He had acquired a special bicycle ergometer that he could use from his wheelchair; it strengthened his leg muscles.

The publisher called and invited him to visit them to get to know everyone there. They paid for train tickets for him and Juno.

Jupiter would soon need to order the wheelchair lift for the train, perhaps it would come too late again. But Juno would stop the ICE again as she did before, when they were going to the literature contest in Berlin, stamping her foot and bellowing through the train station.

Juno showed Jupiter photos of the rehearsals for the *Pas de Quatre*. Wonderful, said Jupiter.

Juno told him that she had already asked Hippolyta on the first floor whether she would be at home on the day of the performance and if she could help her, because of the steps. And she said she would help.

There were two steps on the outside of the theatre.

I called; they'll carry you up in your wheelchair, said Juno.

Juno wished for the performance. But truthfully, she wished even more that the rehearsals would never end. The time when you were living towards something big was actually what you could call normal life. When you were preparing something.

For the duration of the *Pas de Quatre*, she would hold the hands of Maria, Carlotta, Fanny, Lucile, but also of Daphne, Ursi and Athena. Time didn't exist as a line, but as a soup.

They were the quartet of eternal life, no dates applied to them, in this chamber with mirrors that reflected the light so that they all looked young for ever, and they were too.

The thing with time and ageing had long since been disproven.

You could see this in them, the dancers, that they stop time, or they can move through it, as you could theoretically just move through the CERN tubes and nothing would happen; nothing would stop or die, just a particle slipped into Juno's body. It was Marie Taglioni's gene that Juno carried inside her.

Juno was so lively that she took off.
She was just there, dancing with her friends, she was whirling around and doing pirouettes and jumping in quick glissades assemblés from left to right and back again.
Naïs, the teacher, shot them through the CERN tubes.
They were particles that did not belong to anyone.
That didn't stick anywhere.

Her life didn't even belong to her.
It belonged to dance, as you might think.
Even if she didn't always hold the diagonals.

Two additional tattoos were planned for June, a grid of roses and star motifs on her right shoulder, and then a dancer in a flowing dress, Giselle maybe, when she wasn't wearing her country costume any more, but an airy cloud-dress.
This was going on her left calf.
And her life belonged to the theatre as well. At the performances with Phoebus and Tristan in Munich, on all three days they had to go back on stage four times in a row because of the applause. This corresponded to four curtains in a ballet piece.

As long as I play, nothing happens.
Do you hear that, Jupiter?
Do you hear that, Benu?
That's why we always have to keep playing.
As long as I'm playing, nothing happens.

At some point, this slogan would have to go on one of her over-a-metre-long legs.

Juno loved her legs.

Epilogue

June 2023, 11 p.m. Sky cloudy, no constellations. The 'pling' of WhatsApp. Juno was already in bed.

> Hi, how's it going?
> *Smiley*

It was Benu. It used to be Benu.

Benu had a new profile picture, still his face, but it looked eerie, a young man, completely smooth.

He had once had forehead wrinkles and eye wrinkles, he looked at least like he was in his mid-thirties, but now he looked like someone in an embarrassing influencer video.

Furthermore, his skin was much lighter, nearly white.

It may have been the new TikTok filter that made a thirty-year-old teenager out of him.

> Hi, I'm doing really well.

> *Smiley*
> You look really beautiful.
> I fell in love with your profile picture right away.
> *Red heart*

> It's nice of you to say that.

Smiley with the heart-eyes
Where do you live?

> I live in Italy, I'm a prima ballerina. Soon
> I'm going to London,
> We have a premiere.
> I'm Marie Taglioni, by the way.

A beautiful name.
I like it a lot.
Are you married?

Juno blocked the profile.

A Word of Thanks

I worked on this novel for just a little longer than one year. This period was very intense, and many wonderful people supported me and my work during this time.

I thank my husband, Jan Kuhlbrodt, for being there. And not only for not objecting to being confused with Jupiter in this book, but for even thinking that that might be nice. And I thank my beloved daughters, Sofia and Maria, for being on Earth.

I thank my ballet friends, Kumi, Uli and Natalie, as well as my teacher, Tamae Moriyama, for dancing with me and for the *Pas de Quatre* (for ever, your Marie Taglioni). I thank Timm Völker and Patrice Lipeb for appearing, playing, rehearsing and reading with me, and for their friendship and the wonderful radio play that we made from the beginning of *Hey, Good Morning* . . . You're the best.

Sincere thanks to my whole giant family, for laughing, coffee breaks, being there for one another. I thank my mother for her love and for her *Ziegernudeln*.

Thank you also to Spruehling689, Werktags and Mansiehtsichmal for the great tattoos. They are eternal.

I thank Yevgeniy Breyger for everything and for his texts.

A huge thank you also to Matthias Landwehr for believing in this novel from the very beginning. I thank him and his colleagues for their support.

I thank Tom Kraushaar and the whole team at my wonderful publisher, Klett-Cotta, for the heartfelt, understanding assistance, and especially my outstanding copy-editor Katharina Körber for this sparkling, productive, beautiful exchange. And for the phrase 'wild bee-ultra'.

I am grateful to my translator Linda Gaus, my editor Ella Harold and the team at Fig Tree, for all their work to make my novel available to English-speaking readers.

And thank you to the residence of Schauspiel Leipzig, Thomas Frank and Melanie Albrecht, as well as my team from SOFT WAR, a performance that relies on parts of this novel. Thanks to Patrice, Clara, Philipp, Michèle!

Extra-large thanks to Patrice Lipeb, with whom I talked about racism throughout the entire time I was writing this novel, and who, while performing a sensitivity read, made such wise and thoughtful suggestions and alerted me to hidden power traps and discrimination of which I was not aware. This trusting cooperation was an enriching and important experience. Language can reveal 'weak points' in our thinking, which we wouldn't always notice by ourselves.

And last but not least, thank you to anyone who could be Benu. Wherever he is now, whatever he's doing: Hey, you out there, how are you doing? *Smiley*.